Rock Solid

NEW YORK TIMES BESTSELLING AUTHORS
CARLY PHILLIPS
ERIKA WILDE

New York Times Bestselling Authors Carly Phillips and Erika Wilde bring you a new fun, flirty, standalone romance.

Connor Prescott doesn't do one night stands (yes, ladies, he's an anomaly) so when he meets a beautiful woman during a snowed in night at the airport who wants to forget her heartache, he makes an exception. Their night together is incendiary, and by morning Connor wants more . . . except his sexy stranger is gone. He's pretty sure he'll never see her again, until three and a half years later she finds *him*, and changes his entire world with three little words . . .

You're a daddy.

* * *

This book is a work of fiction. Names, characters, places, and incidents either are products of the author's imagination or are used fictitiously. Any resemblance to actual events or locales or persons, living or dead, is entirely coincidental.

Chapter One

Valentine's Day, three years and seven months ago.

SHE CAUGHT HIS eye the moment she sat across from him in the Denver airport terminal. It wasn't her gorgeous blonde hair or her long, slender legs or the hourglass curve of her waist and hips or even the firm, ample breasts shaped beneath the long-sleeve turtle-neck top that held Connor Prescott's attention. No, it was her big, dark brown eyes and her tentative smile as their gazes met for a brief second before she glanced down at the cell phone in her hand.

That quick glimpse at her pretty face was just enough for him to catch the subtle heart-ache in her expression that no woman ought to be feeling on Valentine's Day, and he found himself curious as to what had caused that show of vulnerable emotion.

While she scrolled through her phone with a slight frown marring her brows, he looked at her left hand. There wasn't a ring on her finger, but that didn't mean she wasn't already taken. But it definitely gave him a bit of hope that maybe they could get to know each other better, because with the snowstorm rolling into Denver that afternoon, he had a feeling it was going to be a long night at the airport.

They hadn't cancelled his flight to Chicago, where he lived. Yet. But Connor was pretty sure that's where things were headed, especially with the snow flurries starting outside. The incoming flight to this gate was already delayed, and by the time it landed and passengers disembarked, he was betting that the airport would have made the decision to stop all flights for the night.

It was supposed to be one of those quick and dirty blizzards, the kind that dumped a good twelve to twenty inches of snow in a short period of time. Most likely, by tomorrow in the late afternoon or evening, the runways would be cleared, the planes deiced, flights would have resumed their regular schedules, and the thousands of people at the airport would be scrambling to rebook their seats to their destination.

But for now, it was a sit-and-wait situation. Maybe they'd get out before everything was shut down . . . and maybe not.

He returned his attention to the stranger sitting across from his seat, just in time to see her avert her gaze away from him and bite her lower lip as she looked at her phone again. He couldn't help the smile that tugged at his mouth. So, she'd been checking him out while he'd been looking out the window at the weather. Definitely a positive sign.

He was just getting ready to strike up a casual conversation, but before he could say anything, she abruptly stood, grabbed the handle of her carry-on luggage, and walked away from the sitting area at their gate. He watched her go—and damn, those black jeans she wore drew his gaze to the perfect, rounded curves of her ass. He debated whether or not to follow and decided against it so he didn't look like a complete stalker. Most likely, she was going to the ladies' room and would return in a few minutes.

Except she didn't come back. Half an hour later, his cell phone buzzed with an alert from the airlines, notifying him that his flight had been cancelled. No big surprise there. That message was followed by an announcement over the intercom informing travelers that the entire airport was now shut down until tomorrow morning, or afternoon, depending on how fast the storm blew through. He was stuck in Denver for at least another twenty-four hours.

The last thing Connor wanted to do was sleep on one of the uncomfortable chairs or on the floor with a few thousand other people. He quickly got online, looked up the Westin Denver International Airport Hotel, which was connected directly to the airport terminal, and tried to book a room. He could have walked there, but in the twenty minutes it would take to get to the adjoining hotel, he was fairly certain every room would be gone. As it was, the only thing left that he could get was an executive two-bedroom suite, which was a small fortune and more space than he needed, but hey, the guys—his partners at Premier Realty—had elected to send *him* to Denver on company business, so tough shit, he thought, and didn't hesitate to book it.

Room secured, he texted his sister, Natalie—who was supposed to pick him up when he landed—to give her an update on his situation, then waited around another half an hour like an infatuated teenage boy to see if the intriguing stranger came back, only to be met with extreme disappointment.

His stomach growled, reminding him that he'd missed lunch and he was no longer just hungry but starved. He picked up his travel bag and headed down the concourse toward the hotel, trying to decide where to eat. Every place was jam-packed since so many people were stranded, and he didn't want crappy fast food. Being served a substantial burger and a beer was his preference before he checked into his room for the rest of the afternoon and night.

He came across Boulder Beer Tap House, and bingo, he'd found his restaurant. He made his way inside and was told he could seat himself—and he would have if there had been room at the bar or a vacant table anywhere in the place.

And then fate smiled upon him. Sitting alone at a small, two-seat table in the corner of the restaurant was his beautiful blonde. And the fact that she was eating a burger and drinking a glass of beer, well, he was almost in love because she was *his* kind of girl. Unassuming.

Down-to-earth. Unpretentious. A woman who enjoyed a hearty meal and a dark ale over a diet-conscious salad and a frilly cocktail.

Allowing a charming smile to curve his lips, he started in her direction. After taking a bite of her burger, she wiped her mouth with her napkin as she glanced up, clearly looking right at him as he approached. He didn't miss the awareness that flashed through her eyes or the subtle attraction as her gaze took in the width of his muscled chest beneath the navy blue long-sleeve Henley he wore. Surprisingly, her appraisal didn't stop there . . . No, it did a slow, appreciative perusal down the rest of his body, then back up again.

He was a big guy. Everywhere. Tall and solidly built from manual labor, with linebacker shoulders he'd put to good use in college and long legs that completed his six-foot-five frame. He'd already estimated that he was close to six inches taller than she was the moment she stood up back at the gate, and he could easily imagine how perfectly she'd fit against him, in all the right places.

By the time he'd reached her table, her head was tipped back to look up at his face, her eyes wide with surprise that he'd sought her out.

And then she absently licked her bottom lip, and fuck, the action was so guileless, and so damn hot. His dick twitched at the thought of that sexy mouth and that soft, pink tongue wrapped around his cock. Jesus, it had been a long time since he'd had such a visceral reaction to a woman . . . and he welcomed it . . . and sent up a small prayer in hopes that she was single so he could pursue the chemistry that was clearly mutual.

She was still staring at him with those big brown eyes, curious and unsure, and he broke the silence hanging between them. "The place is a little busy and you've got the only free seat in the house," he said, indicating the vacant chair across from her. "Mind if I join you?"

She paused for a moment, just long enough for Connor to catch a quick glimmer of wariness and uncertainty in her expression. He braced himself for a rejection—there was obviously something going on with her—but then she gave her head a shake and the emotions cleared.

"I'm sorry," she said, her cheeks flushing with embarrassment. "I just . . . You caught me off guard. Of course you can join me. Have a seat." The warm, sweet smile she gave him made up for her previous hesitation.

He grinned back at her as he settled himself in the wooden chair and dropped his duffel bag at his feet. "I'm Connor," he said, stretching his hand across the table toward her—to introduce himself, and because selfishly, he wanted to touch her and *feel* the connection between them.

She quickly wiped her hand on her napkin, looking adorably chagrined as she returned the gesture. "Sorry, my fingers are kind of greasy from the burger. I'm Katie."

"No worries. I'm all about a good greasy burger." He shook her hand, holding on a little longer than necessary, enjoying the softness of her skin and the slight hitch to her breath and the flare of awareness in her gaze as he skimmed his calloused thumb across her knuckles before letting go.

"It's a pleasure to meet you, Katie," he said, releasing her hand. "Thank you for letting me crash your meal. I'm starved and it's obviously going to be a long night."

"True," she agreed, revealing she was also aware of the airport shutting down for the night. "And I really don't mind sharing the table, though I can't guarantee that I'm great company right now, so I apologize ahead of time if I'm not very . . . personable."

Which explained the range of emotions she'd already displayed thus far. "Bad day?" he asked, tipping his head curiously.

She glanced down at her plate and tried for a casual shrug, but it was weighted by something much heavier. "Yeah, you could say that."

He waited for her to say more, but she didn't, and then their waitress came by the table, clearly frazzled by how slammed the restaurant was.

"Do you need a menu?" she asked Connor.

"Nope." Wanting to make things as easy as possible for the stressed-out server, he pointed to Katie's plate. "I'll have exactly what she's having. The burger *and* the beer."

"And I'll have another one of these," Katie said, tapping her nearly empty glass of ale.

"Thank you," the young girl said, relieved that they'd given her a simple and straightforward order before she moved on to the more demanding customers sitting at the next table.

He returned his attention to the lovely woman sitting across from him as she finished off her beer. "So, you come here often?" Yeah, it was a cheesy line, but it was a good icebreaker.

The corner of her mouth quirked with amusement. "To this restaurant, or Denver?"

He chuckled as he leaned back in his chair, liking this feistier side to her personality. It was so much better than the wariness. "Denver," he clarified. "Do you live here or are you leaving after a visit?" It was a casual question, but he'd be lying if he said he wasn't fishing for more personal information, because it would be much easier to see her again if they at least lived in the same city.

Yeah, he was already thinking that far ahead, because there was something about Katie that sparked an interest he hadn't felt in what seemed like forever. It was that combination of sweetness along with the few glimpses of vulnerability he'd already seen that fascinated him and stirred that protective nature of his. He wasn't sure *why* she evoked those emotions, but it was enough for him to want to pursue her and see where it might lead.

The humor he'd coaxed from her moments ago evaporated. "I'm leaving Denver . . . after being utterly humiliated," she admitted. "I'm heading back to Chicago, where I live, because I seriously need to reassess my life and make some changes."

Her unexpected reply took him aback and had him wondering what, exactly, had happened to her. Katie's fluctuating emotions now made sense, but he could tell there was a whole lot more to her story. Just when he decided to ask, their waitress came by with their beers and his hamburger, stealing the moment away from him.

As well as giving Katie the opportunity to redirect the conversation. "What about you?" she asked before taking a drink of her chilled beer.

Clearly, she wasn't going to elaborate on those life changes she felt compelled to make. There was no doubt that Connor wanted to know her secrets, but he also wanted her to share them freely. "I was here on business attending a conference on real estate investments," he told her as he piled the lettuce, tomato, and pickles on the thick meat patty, then pressed the bun back on top before picking up the burger for a big bite.

He chewed, swallowed, and continued. "I live in Chicago, as well." Then he gave her a sympathetic look. "And I'm really sorry about whatever happened to humiliate you."

She leaned back in her chair, her pained expression quickly becoming eclipsed by a slow-building anger as she considered the situation. "Honestly, I should have seen it coming."

"Seen what coming?" he asked after another bite, gently providing her with the opportunity to open up, because he could see that she was struggling with the desire to give that frustration inside of her some kind of outlet.

Lips pursed, she shook her head and glanced away. "Trust me, it's a long, completely embarrassing story that no guy wants to hear."

"Try me." She remained skeptical, and he was suddenly determined to prove her wrong about him not caring about her bad day. "I've got all night. Literally. And so do you, now that our flight has been cancelled. And if it makes you feel any better, I swear that whatever you say in Denver will absolutely stay in Denver." Grinning at her, he made a small cross over his heart with his index finger to seal the promise, and counted the tiny peek of a smile that appeared on her lips as a small victory.

"You're very . . . persuasive."

He shrugged as he finished off his burger, his appetite sated for now. Pushing aside his plate, he braced his forearms on the table in front of him. "Honestly, I just think it might help to get whatever is bothering you off your chest. Blow off some steam and release all that stress and aggravation so you can breathe again without feeling like someone is sitting on your chest."

She nodded absently. "It does feel that way," she admitted.

"No pressure," he said, putting both his hands up in an easygoing gesture, though he wasn't below trying a little reverse psychology. "But I also understand if it's something you don't want to discuss."

She tipped her head to the side and eyed him perceptively as he took a drink of his beer. "You're a stranger, and I don't even know you, at least not well enough to share something so personal with you."

He was hoping to change all that over the course of their time together, which was at least the next twenty-four hours. "Even better, don't you think? Who am I going to tell your story to that it'll matter?"

"That's true," she murmured, seemingly considering his offer to listen. As she thought it over and drank her second beer, he watched as she sat up a bit straighter in her chair and her chin lifted with a spark of rebellion.

"You know what? You're right," she said, her voice firm and determined, matching the sudden flash of defiance that lit her eyes. "I *do* want to talk about it, because I'm so done letting that jerk make me feel like what happened is all *my* fault when he's the one who screwed up."

He raised his brows in surprise over her pronouncement, but there was no denying he really liked this new, gutsy attitude of hers. "Okay, let's hear it."

She downed the rest of her beer, probably for extra fortitude, Connor guessed. "I came to Denver to surprise my boyfriend of eight months for Valentine's Day because I *thought* he was on a business trip this weekend and would hopefully have the evening free. And since things have been strained between us, and more than a little . . . lackluster in the bedroom lately, I thought I'd surprise him and spice things up with some fantasy sex."

That was the last thing he'd expected her to say and he tipped his head to the side curiously. "Fantasy sex?" he asked, dying to know what she deemed a worthy fantasy.

The color on her cheeks pinkened, but much to his delight, she didn't back down from the question. "You know, role playing. The whole sex-with-a-stranger thing in a hotel room. It sounded fun and exciting and I stupidly thought it was just what we needed to get our relationship back on track again."

He almost hated to ask . . . "But?"

Her lips pursed for a moment. "But when I knocked on his door, he answered with a towel around his waist. His hair was wet, like he'd just gotten out of the shower, and I could still hear the water running in the bathroom. And of course he was shocked to see me because me being there *was* supposed to be a surprise, so his startled expression didn't seem out of place. He blurted out that he thought I was the room service he'd ordered, and he wouldn't step aside to let me in, which confused me at first."

She paused, and Connor let out an empathetic groan, because he knew exactly where this story was heading and how it was going to end. He also knew the anger and pain of finding out that someone you were in a relationship with had betrayed your trust. He'd been there, done that, and it fucking sucked.

Katie shifted in her seat and bravely went on, even though he knew how difficult this next part had to be for her to say out loud. "So, while we're standing there staring at each other, with me waiting for him to show some kind of sign that he was happy to see me, the shower in the bathroom turned off. And again, I stupidly thought, 'How in the world did that happen when Brice was standing right in front of me?', and then a woman with her own towel wrapped around her came into view and answered that question."

Connor had known the outcome, but he swore beneath his breath anyway, because the hurt in her eyes made him want to punch Brice in the goddamn face for being a lying, cheating douchebag—and for humiliating Katie, instead of ending a relationship he obviously didn't want to be in. Not to mention the damage to Katie's dignity and self-esteem as a woman.

She wasn't crying. Her eyes were dry, but that didn't mean she wasn't feeling devastated. Then again, maybe she hadn't been invested in Brice as much as she'd thought, either.

"So, once I got over *my* shock at realizing he was having an affair while on his business trip, Brice proceeded to tell me that he hasn't been feeling it for a while now with me, and he was done. He didn't display an ounce of guilt, and the only apology I got from him was that he was sorry I came all the way to Denver for nothing. Happy freaking Valentine's Day to me, huh?" She met Connor's gaze and shook her head. "I was a naive idiot for thinking that this surprise trip would magically make all our problems disappear."

Without really thinking about his actions, he reached across the table and grabbed her hand, enveloping it in his so she didn't feel so alone. "You weren't an idiot, Katie. He's a selfish prick. If he wasn't 'feeling it,' then he should have ended things with you before sticking his pencil dick into another woman."

An unexpected snort of laughter escaped her, and instead of looking mortified at the slip, she laughed again, as if deferring to humor was just the right medicine she needed at this moment. "You're right again. He's an asshole and he doesn't deserve me anyway. And 'pencil dick' isn't too far from the truth, either." Then she grinned. "Damn, that felt good."

He smiled, too, glad to see her bounce back, though he knew it didn't erase the humiliation she'd endured. "It's the truth, Katie, and you're going to be okay." He knew that from experience, too.

"Yeah, I know," she said on a sigh. "Like I

said, in hindsight, I should have seen something like this coming. Now, I just want to get back to Chicago and pack up all his stuff from my place so I never have to see him again. Unfortunately, it's going to be a long night, hanging out in the airport with too much free time to think and trying to find somewhere comfortable to sleep. I was really looking forward to a long, hot shower at home and being in my own bed tonight."

Connor *really* tried not to think of Katie in either of those situations—naked in a shower with water running down her luscious, curvy body or her lying back on a comforter, that gorgeous hair of hers spread out over her pillow and her full, kissable lips parted as she slept— but his misbehaving brain had a mind of its own and had no issues projecting those sexy images in his head.

Okay, now who was the asshole? He had no business lusting over Katie when she'd just been dumped by her boyfriend, in quite an offensive way. In fact, he needed to show her there were some men who could be a gentleman, and Connor would like to think that was one of his better qualities. And even though his mind might have conjured up a hot, sexy scenario with Katie in the starring role, that's all it really was . . . just a harmless fantasy that he might or might not think about when he got into bed tonight, closed his eyes, and wrapped his hand around his hard, aching—

"I wonder if the Westin has any rooms left for the night," she said, putting a screeching halt on his thoughts as she retrieved her phone from her handbag to give them a call.

"Doubtful. They were pretty limited when I called about forty minutes ago to book my room." Which reminded him that his suite had *two* bedrooms. "But lucky for you, I have a soft, comfortable bed you can sleep on and a nice hot shower to go with it."

Her gaze jerked to his, and too late he realized just how suggestive his words sounded . . . like he was offering to share *his* bed with her. But right after the comment left his mouth, and before he could explain what he meant, their waitress stopped at their table.

"Can I get the two of you anything else?" she asked.

Connor glanced across the table at Katie, her eyes still wide as she shook her head to answer the waitress's question.

"I think we're both good," he said, and as

soon as the girl set the two separate checks on the table, he reached for them both and pulled out his wallet.

"Umm, I can pay for my own meal," Katie told him.

After what he'd just said, she probably thought he was buying her dinner because he expected her to put out in return. But that wasn't the case. He was just trying to be a nice guy and implement the manners his parents had drilled into him as a teenager.

"I'm paying for your meal because my father would kick my ass if I didn't," he explained with humor, and when her brows creased in confusion, he clarified further. "As soon as I was old enough to date, my dad taught me that it was my obligation as a man to pick up the tab when dining with a woman, because it was the polite, courteous thing to do. It doesn't mean there are any strings or expectations attached," he said, wanting to make that clear. "It's just what I've always done, and now it's a habit that's pretty much ingrained."

"Oh, okay," she said, her expression softening. "Thank you, then."

"It's my pleasure," he said as he placed enough bills on the table to cover both checks, along with a generous tip, before addressing his earlier faux pas.

He lifted his gaze to hers more seriously. "So, about that offer I just made about a room . . . before you think I'm a total creep who just propositioned you, let me clarify that all the Westin Hotel had available when I called was a two-bedroom suite, and I booked it because I wasn't about to hang out and sleep in the terminal until the storm passes. So, considering the day you've had, I'd like to offer you the extra room to stay in."

She hesitated, which he understood, before asking, "Are you sure?"

He didn't miss the hopeful note in her voice, and he discovered he liked being her white knight, the guy who came to her rescue after her dumb-ass boyfriend's stupidity in letting her go. "I'm one hundred percent certain. Besides, it'll be nice to have a roommate for the next twenty-four hours. We can celebrate Valentine's Day together by watching cheesy movies on pay-per-view all night and gorging on all the junk food in the mini bar, then sleep off the sugar coma all tomorrow morning."

She returned his grin, her eyes sparkling

with delight. "Ahhh, cheesy movies and junk food. You sure do know how to sweet-talk a girl," she teased.

He laughed as he pushed his chair back and stood. "And to think that you haven't even seen some of my best moves yet," he said with a flirtatious wink as he picked up his duffel and grabbed the handle of her luggage before she could. "Come on, Valentine. Let's blow this joint and get our slumber party started."

Chapter Two

FROM THE MOMENT her boyfriend—make that *ex*-boyfriend—closed the door on her after so coldly ending their relationship, Katie Kaswell wouldn't have thought that her shitty day could take a turn for the better. But it had, in the form of a gorgeous guy who was hotter than Hades, with a devastatingly sexy smile that made her stomach flutter in sensual awareness because everything about him was so easygoing and charming—the exact opposite of Brice's more uptight and narcissistic personality, which she'd seen in all its glory earlier today.

As they walked side by side through the airport terminal and toward the Westin Hotel, she cast a surreptitious look at the man who'd generously offered her a place to stay for the night without any expectations. She'd only known Connor for an hour, but there was nothing egotistical about him that she'd detected so far, nor had he come off as a player looking for a snowstorm hookup, which had been her first thought when he'd asked to sit at her table.

Instead, he'd been kind and sympathetic while she'd shared her humiliating situation with him, listening attentively to her story, whereas most guys would have been completely uninterested in the reason behind her unpleasant mood. He'd even managed to make her feel *better* about the whole mortifying experience, calling Brice a selfish prick with a pencil dick. Remembering his comment almost made her laugh out loud all over again.

They wove in and out of the crowd of people stuck at the airport, and Katie didn't miss the way a lot of women eyed Connor appreciatively as they walked by, even a few who appeared to be with a significant other. Not that she blamed any of them for admiring what a gorgeous, virile male he was. He was big and tall, with thick, dark brown hair, stunning blue eyes, and a rock-hard body built for sin. And that light scruff on his jaw? So. Damn. Hot.

The man was sex on two legs, though he seemed completely oblivious to the ogling stares, whereas most guys would have upped their swagger to try and further impress their female audience. No, there was nothing cocky or arrogant about him, and she found that was incredibly appealing, too.

During their meal together, he'd pushed up the sleeves of his navy blue Henley, treating her—and every other woman in the vicinity—to his strong forearms and the sexy tattoos that covered one of his arms all the way down to the back of his hand. That intriguing ink increased his hotness factor by at least another ten points. It also made her wonder what he'd look like with his shirt completely off and what his skin would feel like sliding against the tips of her fingers and how the muscles in his chest might react to the caress of her hands all the way down to his stomach.

Her pulse skipped a beat, and that spark of attraction that had been missing with Brice, especially over the last few months, came back with a vengeance, showing her body just how wonderful, *how exciting*, desire could feel. That heady awareness tightened her nipples and curled seductively through her belly, then settled between her thighs, surprising her.

Oh, hello, arousal. That's where you've been!

A small smile touched her lips as they headed into the Westin. After the spectacular way Brice had humiliated her, along with making her feel as though their lackluster sex life had been her fault, she didn't even experience a sliver of guilt for her physical reaction to Connor. No, she found it exhilarating and, oddly enough, empowering. Kind of like a big ol' *fuck you* to Brice, that it had taken mere thoughts of another man to make her body feel like a woman again.

Connor walked to the sitting area in the lobby and put her luggage and his duffel next to a vacant chair. "Mind hanging here with our bags while I check in? No sense both of us standing in that long line when you can be comfortable sitting here."

Her gaze traveled from the crowd of people waiting to register for their rooms, then back to Connor as she gave him a smile, appreciating his courteous gesture. "No, I don't mind at all."

Yeah, she was totally fine with that decision, especially when he walked away and she got her first good look at his backside. Broad shoulders. Narrow waist. And a firm ass hugged by a pair of fitted jeans. The man was an Adonis. Physically flawless and thoughtful, to boot. Which made her wonder why some woman hadn't already snatched him up . . . unless he liked being a bachelor.

Forty minutes later, Connor returned and handed her a keycard of her own, just in case she needed it, he told her. They rode the elevator up to the very top floor, and she followed him to their room, then inside once he had the door open. The suite was wide and spacious, with a living room and kitchen in the middle and a master bedroom with an adjoining bathroom on either side of those main rooms.

He dropped his bag on the couch, then rolled her luggage into one of the bedrooms and parked it next to the bed before facing her with an easy smile that belied the flicker of heat in his eyes as his gaze briefly dipped down to her mouth. Now that they were alone, *really alone*, something in the air between them seemed to shift, bringing with it a seductive pull she was suddenly finding difficult to resist. Connor was that temptation, and she couldn't stop from wondering what would happen if she stepped closer and touched him. If she lifted her mouth to his for a kiss just so she could see what he tasted like and what it would be like to have him *not* be such a gentleman.

He pushed his fingers into the front pockets of his jeans, as if he was having an equally difficult time keeping his hands to himself and needed to keep them restrained. "Here you go. A soft, comfortable bed for the night and that hot shower you wanted," he finally said, his voice a bit rough around the edges despite his polite words. "And if you just want to crawl into bed and fall asleep, I totally understand. But if you'd rather have some company and you're interested in taking me up on that offer of cheesy movies and junk food, I'll be hanging out in the living room."

He turned to go, and she stopped him before he could leave. "Connor?"

He glanced back, his expression unreadable. "Yeah?"

"I just wanted to thank you, for listening when I needed to vent," she said, needing him to know how much she appreciated him being so kind and caring after her craptastic afternoon. "You're a really nice guy, which is hard to come by these days." She ought to know, considering her track record with the *wrong* kind of men.

The corner of his mouth twitched with a wry grin that mocked the compliment she'd just given him. "Yeah, well, sometimes being a nice guy is way overrated."

He exited the room and closed the door quietly behind him, his parting remark revealing that keeping his hands to himself might not be as easy as he made it look. That he was quite possibly struggling between being respectful because of her breakup with Brice and giving in to the attraction they both clearly felt.

She understood the physical tug-of-war, because she was experiencing it, too.

Exhaling a deep breath, she grabbed her toiletry bag and headed into the adjoining bathroom and stripped out of her clothes. Turning on the shower, she pinned up her hair, then stepped beneath the spray, letting the hot water wash away the last of the day's hurt and anger. Brice wasn't worth the emotion, and if she was honest with herself, her heart wasn't broken, because in her gut, she'd known for at least the past two months that her relationship with Brice was heading toward *the end*.

As always, the foreshadowing had been there. Him working longer, later hours. Canceling plans at the last minute. Being distracted on his phone when they were together and telling her it was business when she asked who he was texting with. But instead of heeding those signs, Katie did what she'd always done. She'd given Brice the benefit of the doubt, hoping that for once, her intuition was wrong. She'd hung in there, never wanting to feel as though she didn't at least try to make things work, because she'd always sworn she wouldn't treat relationships like her parents did—like they were disposable.

But in the end, Katie's efforts and determination never paid off, and she was always the one on the receiving end of an *it's not me, it's you* speech, for one reason or another. Just like her previous two relationships before Brice, she'd been dumped once the excitement and shininess wore off, and it always left her feeling as though she wasn't worth the effort. That she wasn't *enough*.

That was the painful part, because she'd grown up feeling that way with her mother and father. She'd been used as a pawn in her parents' divorce, depending on what either of them wanted from the other at any given time, but once they managed to achieve their objective, their attention abruptly ended until the next time one of them needed her for some kind of leverage.

From the young age of four, that continuous push-pull had been her life with her parents, until she finally graduated high school and could move to another state for college and neither one of them could manipulate her emotions any longer. Unfortunately, that childhood had carried over into adulthood and her relationships with men. She was always too eager to please, even at the expense of her own happiness, and it always came back to bite her in the ass.

Clearly, she couldn't trust her judgment when it came to the opposite sex. And clearly, it was time to reevaluate her life and focus on being content without a man who would eventually disappoint her like all the others had.

Pushing all those thoughts from her head, she finished up in the shower, rinsing the frothy body wash from her skin and turning off the water before she turned into a prune. Grabbing a towel, she dried off, then wrapped it around her as she walked back into the bedroom to get dressed.

But as she looked through her suitcase, she came across the lingerie she'd bought as a Valentine's Day surprise for Brice, which was all she'd intended to wear for the weekend—that or nothing at all—other than her jeans outside of the hotel room. The risqué nightie in her hand mocked her for being a fool, and she suddenly wanted to forget about her embarrassing afternoon and erase Brice from her mind completely tonight.

She thought about Connor waiting in the living room for her, and her pulse beat slow and thick in her veins as his final comment came back to taunt her . . . *being a nice guy is way overrated.*

He didn't *want* to be a nice guy. That much she knew. What he wanted was *her*, and after having her self-esteem take such a direct hit, the notion of feeling sexy and desirable, even for one night, was so tempting. The last thing she wanted right now was a commitment or forever promises when that clearly was not her forte, but hot, mindless sex with a gorgeous, hot-as-hell stranger she'd never see again? Yeah, that sounded absolutely perfect and exactly what *she* needed.

Gathering the fortitude to go through with her plan, she let the towel drop to the floor and put on the red lace baby-doll top and matching panties before she changed her mind. She unclipped her hair and let it fall to her shoulders, then ruffled her fingers through the strands to give her a more tousled, just-rolled-out-of-bed kind of look. She touched up her makeup and dabbed her lips with a tinted moisturizing balm.

Her stomach was a bundle of crazy wild nerves, but there was also something incredibly exhilarating about being so spontaneous when she was the kind of woman who'd always planned things out. But look where *that* had gotten her . . . stuck in a snowstorm in Denver after finding out her ex had been screwing someone else.

But it had also gotten her stranded with Connor, and for once in her life, Katie was going to be impulsive and enjoy whatever tonight and the *nice guy* out in the living room had to offer.

CONNOR SCROLLED THROUGH the list of movies on pay-per-view for the tenth time, not sure what Katie might be in the mood for. He'd raided the mini bar as promised, and all the junk food loot was on the coffee table awaiting their impromptu slumber party. He was just waiting, albeit impatiently, to find out if Katie was going to join him or not. After her emotionally draining day, he wasn't sure she was going to be up to hanging out, and as much as he'd understand that decision, the thought mostly disappointed him.

When he heard the door to her bedroom open, a flood of relief coursed through him. "So, what are you in the mood for?" he asked, anxious for her to join him and hoping that she sat on the same sofa as he did instead of the single chair opposite the couch—*Jesus, what was he, fourteen?* "We've got our choice between a romantic comedy, action adventure, or a horror flick."

"None of those," she said, her voice soft and husky as she approached from his peripheral vision. "The only thing I'm in the mood for is . . . you."

Certain that he'd heard Katie wrong, he turned his head to glance at her. His jaw dropped open in shock as he stared at the stunning, erotic vision standing a few feet away from him, dressed in a sinful red ensemble that screamed *fuck me, please.* Unsure as to what was going on—was he being cruelly punked right now?—his entire body went rigid, including his dick, as he desperately tried to clear the lust that was quickly fogging his brain.

He managed to close his mouth, but that only made his jaw clench achingly tight as he fought off the urge to do something stupid, like push her down to the couch and give free rein to the attraction they'd both been skirting. Jesus, he couldn't tear his eyes away from her and the see-through lingerie that exposed more than it covered, teasing him mercilessly. The sheer underwire cups pushed her generous breasts up like an offering, barely containing all that mouthwatering fullness, and her tight, rosy nipples pushed against the thin, lacy fabric. The skirt of the short gown draped over her midsection like a veil, sheer enough for him to see the indentation of her waist and flare of her hips, and a pair of tiny red matching panties he wanted to tear off of her with his teeth.

He swore beneath his breath, and when she made a soft, uncertain noise in the back of her throat, he jerked his gaze back up to hers. He caught a quick glimpse of apprehension shimmering in those big brown eyes, which contradicted the bold, brazen woman currently standing in front of him.

"Maybe this was a really stupid idea," she

said in a voice that cracked with a wealth of doubts, right before she turned back around and rushed toward her bedroom in a blur of red material that swirled around her waist and thighs.

Realizing that she believed his hesitation was because he didn't want her, Connor jumped to his feet and reached Katie before she made it halfway across the living room. He caught her around the waist with a strong arm and hauled her up against his body, her back to his front—and quickly realized what a huge mistake *that* was.

She valiantly struggled to break free of his hold, the curve of her delectable ass shifting and wriggling against the thick length of his cock already straining the zipper of his jeans. He gritted his teeth at the onslaught of lust racing through his blood, threatening to eradicate his self-control and any rational decisions he needed to make. And the situation definitely called for him to remain level-headed so he could think with his brain and not his unruly dick.

She tried to push away his arm one last time, but when it didn't budge, she made a frustrated sound. "Just let me go, Connor," she said, her voice defeated and so damn vulnerable. "*Please.*"

He wasn't releasing her until he knew she was okay. "Katie—"

"Don't make this any worse than it already is," she said, cutting him off, her entire body still unyielding against his. "I must have misread your interest, and I don't think I can handle getting rejected twice in one day."

Aww, fuck. The very last thing he felt for her was disinterest, but he didn't want to take advantage of her or the situation, either. He released her and turned Katie so that she was facing him, hating the wariness in her gaze. She looked like she was going to bolt again, and he wasn't about to let that happen until they got a few things straight. With his hands gripping her hips so she couldn't go anywhere, at least not easily, he backed her up a few steps, until she was trapped between him and the wall.

The impulse to run his hands up the indentation of her waist to the breasts nearly spilling out of her flimsy top was so strong and so distracting he had to place his palms safely on the wall on either side of her shoulders. She tipped her head back to look up at him, and he nearly smiled when he saw the earlier doubts that had been clouding her gaze were now replaced with a stubborn attitude that turned him on way too much.

"First of all, you didn't misread anything," he told her. "You surprised the fuck out of me, because I didn't expect you to come out of your room looking like a goddamn sex kitten. And secondly, I'm not rejecting you personally."

Her chin lifted obstinately. "Just what I'm offering?"

The corner of his mouth quirked at the impudent tone of her voice, and before he could think better of it, he touched one of the soft, blonde strands of hair that fell to the swell of her breasts. He rubbed the silky texture between his fingers, immediately imagining how it would feel to have his entire hand wrapped around the length. Tugging. Pulling. Her gasping. Moaning. *Begging.*

The heady images in his head fueled his growing hunger for her. "What, exactly, are you offering, Valentine?" he murmured, knowing he was torturing himself but beyond caring any longer.

She rolled her eyes at him. "Isn't it obvious?"

He watched as her tongue dampened her bottom lip, spurring more dirty thoughts to fill his head. "Tell me," he said, the words a gentle demand. "Just so it's clear for both of us."

She hesitated for a moment, as if gathering up the nerve, then spoke. "Remember that fantasy I told you about earlier? The sex-with-a-stranger-in-a-hotel-room fantasy?"

How could he forget something like that? "Yes."

She exhaled a breath. "That's all I want. No last names. No personal information. Just a night of hot, mindless sex."

Yeah, that sounded damn good, except he was already coming to want so much more than that with her. "I'm not really a one-night-stand kind of guy."

It was the truth. Unlike a lot of his friends, he'd never been the type to screw a woman just to get off, without the intention of ever seeing her again. It just wasn't who he was. He liked getting to know the women he slept with, liked the intimacy of learning what gave them the most pleasure so the next time they fucked, it was twice as good because of that connection.

"Care to make an exception?" Holding his gaze, she brazenly slipped her hands beneath the hem of his shirt, her fingers grazing the taut skin right above the waistband of his jeans. "I just want to forget about everything that happened today. I just want to feel good."

He tipped his head. "So, I'm your rebound guy?"

"Would that be so bad?" she asked, tempting him further as her hand dropped lower, finding his weakness and exploiting it . . . his throbbing, aching cock.

Her palm molded to that column of flesh, already as long and hard as a steel rod. And when she squeezed him through the too-tight denim, he had to bite back a strangled groan of need.

"I'm not asking for any promises, Connor. I just want you to fuck me," she said, chipping away at all his good intentions. She raised up on her tiptoes so that her mouth softly, seductively brushed the corner of his. "And judging by the impressive size of your erection, you obviously want the same thing, so please, don't tell me no."

There was only so much teasing a man could take, and she'd just pushed him past his limit. Before he came to his senses—and Jesus, did he really want to deny them both at this point?—he thrust all ten fingers into her hair and around to the back of her head so *he* was now the one in control and sealed his mouth over hers. Her lips parted on a gasp of surprise, and he didn't hesitate to sweep his tongue inside so he could thoroughly taste her. She was hotter and sweeter than he'd imagined, and as the kiss intensified even more, she gripped his shoulders and made the sexiest noises in the back of her throat. Heat rushed through him at the thought of hearing more of those erotic sounds as he buried himself eight inches deep inside of her.

She wanted to fuck? Fine. He'd give her what she wanted, what she needed, without making any personal demands tonight. But tomorrow, before they left Denver and headed home to Chicago, he'd have her last name and number in his cell phone. Because he already knew that one night with Katie wasn't going to be enough, that he'd want more of her and everything her asshole ex had thrown away.

And by morning, she'd realize that, too. He'd make sure of it.

When he finally ended the kiss and lifted his head to look down at her, she was breathing as hard as he was. The desire etching her beautiful features enthralled him. Bringing one hand down to her jaw, he skimmed his thumb along her wet bottom lip, and when she licked the pad of his finger, he felt it all the way down to his cock.

He groaned, knowing if he didn't slow things down, he wasn't going to last long at all. "If we're doing this, we're doing it *my* way," he told her.

She blinked languidly at him. "And what way is that?"

"I want to take my time." He slowly traced a finger down the red lace framing her breasts, watching as her nipples furled tight and hard against the thin fabric. "We've got all night, and I want to enjoy this. I want to enjoy *you*."

"Umm, yes, please," she whispered in agreement.

Taking her hand in his, he led her back to the couch. He sat down and drew her closer. "Straddle my lap, sweetheart."

With his help, she moved over him, settling her knees on either side of his hips and resting her bottom on his thighs. "Will you take off your shirt?" she asked, and he wasn't sure why she'd even bothered to ask permission since her hands were already lifting up the hem of his Henley and shoving it up his chest, clearly eager to rid him of the piece of clothing.

He took over, pulling the shirt over his head

and tossing it aside. He figured it was only fair that he was half-naked, because it wouldn't be long before she was, too.

Her appreciative gaze took in his shoulders and chest as she touched him reverently, hands skimming along his pecs, her thumbs grazing his nipples and her fingers following the taut lines of muscle cutting across his abdomen. She licked her lips like she wanted to put that sultry mouth all over him but didn't know where to start, though he certainly had plenty of ideas.

"God, you are so . . . *everything*," she said, her voice filled with awe.

He slid his palms up her bare arms, her skin so incredibly soft beneath his more calloused, work-roughened fingers. "So everything?" he questioned curiously.

She nodded, those wandering hands of hers feeling up his firm biceps before moving down to his forearms, where her fingers trailed across the tattoos. "So hot. Hard. Gorgeous. Sexy. And *big* in all the places that count," she added with a suggestive smile on her lips. "That is *not* a pencil dick in your pants."

He laughed abruptly at their shared joke. "Not even close," he said, taking credit where it was due.

Pressing his hands between her shoulder blades, he brought her in closer so he could graze his teeth along her shoulder and nuzzle his damp, parted lips against her neck and inhale her arousing feminine scent. He sucked on her supple skin, loving the way she shivered and moaned and arched toward him so uninhibitedly.

His fingers found the thin straps holding up her lingerie, and he dragged them both down her arms. "Your turn to show me your chest," he teased as he sat back against the couch cushion once again and slowly peeled away the lacy material.

His breath hitched in his throat when her perfect tits bounced free. "Jesus Christ, you're stunning," he rasped, and didn't hesitate to fill his hands with all that beauty. He rolled her diamond-hard nipples between his fingers before giving in to the need to taste her. He licked one deliciously stiff peak, swirled his tongue around her areola, and she buried her fingers in his hair, gripping the strands and holding him there while murmuring the words *more, more, more.*

He obliged, his hot, wet mouth taking her deeper, sucking harder, his teeth scraping just enough to add a bit of pleasurable pain that had her whimpering with desire. Her knees locked against his hips, and she rocked against his confined erection, this time chanting *please, please, please.*

He dropped a hand between her spread legs, fully expecting to have to deal with the barrier of her panties... except, fuck, they were *crotchless*, and his fingers slid against her bare pussy, granting him immediate access. A possessive growl tore from Connor's chest, because while Katie might have bought the sexy outfit and underwear for Brice, she'd worn it for *him.*

And Jesus, she was already slick with arousal, making it incredibly easy to sink two fingers into all that tight heat. He rubbed his thumb against her clit, stroking that sensitive flesh rhythmically. Her body shuddered, and she dropped her head to his shoulder, her increasingly erratic breaths blowing hot and damp along the side of his neck. With his free hand, he fisted her thick fall of hair and drew her head back so he could look at her flushed face as he fucked her with his fingers, as he brought her closer to the edge. Her mouth was slack with pleasure, her eyes heavy-lidded with heat and passion as they held his gaze and pleaded for the orgasm he wasn't quite ready to give her.

"Such a sweet, naughty Valentine," he said of the thrilling surprise that had greeted him between her thighs and the ease with which he could touch her and stroke her. "Tonight, this pussy is mine, Katie. All mine. I want to taste it and fuck it and make it feel so damn good."

"Yes," she moaned, moving her hips faster and grinding against his hand more desperately. "Make it feel good, *please*."

Done tormenting her, he crushed his lips to hers, kissing her hard and deep. He increased the pressure and friction of his thumb while quickening the thrusts of his hand to match the sweep of his tongue ravishing her mouth. Her wild, unraveling groan vibrated against his lips, followed by a higher-pitched cry of erotic bliss as her sex pulsed around his fingers and she gave herself over to the intensity of her orgasm.

AN ANNOYING PINGING sound tried to penetrate Connor's sleep-fogged brain. One beep right after the other. Irritating as fuck and demanding his attention when he wanted to keep sleeping because, after an entire night of getting to know Katie in the most physical, intimate sense, his body was, quite literally, worn out. In the best possible way.

Forgetting what had made him stir in the first place, he buried his face back into his pillow, a slow, satisfied grin curving his lips as his mind replayed one of the hottest, sexiest, most fucking phenomenal nights he'd ever spent with a woman. After Katie's first orgasm out in the living room, they'd taken things into the bedroom, where he'd stripped off her lingerie and the rest of his clothes and really gotten down to the business of making her feel so fucking good that no other man would compare.

Luckily, he'd had five condoms in his duffel bag, which had been left there from the last weekend trip he'd taken with his ex over a year ago. He'd been grateful to find them, and they'd made good use of each and every one until well after midnight . . . in the bed when he'd fucked her for the first time, then against the wall with her legs wrapped tight around his waist, on the dining room table after they'd taken a break to eat something substantial from room service, in the shower after they'd gotten carried away with the chocolate-covered strawberries he'd requested with their meal, and again with her bent over the mattress while he'd taken her from behind.

With no more condoms left, they'd both collapsed on his bed, so spent and sated that they'd crashed from sheer physical exhaustion.

His cock twitched with the beginnings of a morning erection as he recalled how bold and shameless she'd been with him. At least in that respect, when it came to what she wanted sexually, she'd been open and honest and held nothing back. And because of that unabashed trust with her body, he already knew what she liked best, how her body responded to certain touches and well-placed caresses, and what it took to make her scream his name when she came long and hard—and took him along for the intoxicating ride.

Not by his choice, he'd played her game . . . no last names. No personal information exchanged. He'd let her have the whole sex-with-a-stranger fantasy, knowing he had the next morning to persuade her to see him again, and not just for a hookup but for a real, getting-to-know-you date.

Ding . . . ding, ding. That noise came again, rousing him for a second time. *What the fuck?*

He rolled to his back and forced his eyes open. The shades on the window had been drawn so the room was dark, which made it difficult to tell if it was still nighttime or morning. He glanced at the space beside him on the bed, where he'd last seen Katie sleeping, but the spot was empty. He wondered if she was already up, or if at some point she'd moved to her own bedroom.

Ding.

More clear-headed now, he realized that the beeping sounds were coming from his cell phone, alerting him to texts. He picked up the device, and the first thing he saw was that it was after ten in the morning. Jesus, he never slept in that late. Unlocking the phone, he squinted against the bright screen as he read the texts . . . all of which were from the Denver airport with updates on the weather, and from the airlines letting him know that flights would resume early that afternoon. His had been rescheduled for 3:20 p.m.

Wanting to make sure that Katie was aware of the new time since they'd been on the same flight back home, he got out of bed and pulled on the jeans he'd left on the floor, then combed his fingers through his unruly hair as he walked into the adjoining living room. It was empty and quiet, and he headed to her bedroom. The door was already open, and when he glanced inside and saw that the bed was still neatly made and her suitcase was nowhere to be found, his stomach pitched with dread because he instinctively knew that she was gone.

A handwritten note from her that he found on the dining table where he'd fucked her only hours ago confirmed that knowledge. *Connor, you were exactly what I needed and more. Thank you for an incredible night. Your Valentine, Katie.*

No phone number. No contact information. Not even a goddamn last name to help him find her back in Chicago.

Jesus, he'd been fucking ghosted. He swore out loud, his chest tightening in disappointment and frustration as he stalked back into his bedroom, determined to find her before they left Denver, because he *knew* she'd felt that connection between them that had been more than just physical lust. Hell, she was probably still on his flight out, and it was that bit of hope that kept him relatively calm as he took a shower, packed up his things, and checked out of the hotel.

He returned to the airport terminal and

headed straight to the new gate number where his plane would board at the designated time, once the runway was cleared of the snow that had fallen overnight, which hadn't been as bad as the news had anticipated. Katie wasn't there, but Connor was hours early for the flight, so he got something to eat, then sat down in the seated area and waited for her to arrive.

The time passed like molasses as he checked out every blonde woman who walked by—none of whom were Katie—until the announcement was finally made over the intercom that it was time to board the plane to Chicago. When his seat section was called, he didn't get in line. In fact, he waited until everyone else had taken their seats on the plane and there was no one left in the terminal but the desk clerks and him.

"Sir, if you're on this flight, you need to board the plane," the woman at the ticket counter said to him. "They'll be locking the doors in the next five minutes to get ready for takeoff."

He nodded reluctantly and finally walked onto the plane, his gaze scanning all the passengers' faces as he made his way to his seat, to make sure he hadn't missed seeing her, but she wasn't on the flight. After stowing his duffel, he settled into his chair and buckled his seat belt, and as the plane taxied down the runway, he was forced to face the fact that Katie didn't want to be found.

Chapter Three

Present day, three years and seven months later . . .

"MOMMY, WHEN ARE we going to Leah's? I want to give her the lollipop we bought for her."

Katie put the last of the vegetables she'd bought at the market into the crisper and glanced at her nearly three-year-old daughter as she shut the refrigerator door. "In a few more minutes, honey. I still have one more bag to empty, and then we'll go. I promise."

Val let out an impatient sigh, because Katie had made it clear that she couldn't have her lollipop until they'd given Leah hers. "Okay," she said, her little legs swinging back and forth as she sat on one of the kitchen chairs.

While Katie finished putting the rest of the

groceries away, Val played with her favorite My Little Pony figurine, Pinkie Pie, on the table. Her little girl carried on an imaginary conversation with the toy, asking Pinkie if she wanted a lick of her lollipop, which was still sealed in its wrapper, and of course the pony had to give it a few loud, slurping licks.

Katie tried not to laugh at the obnoxious sounds her daughter made and the stern way that Val told Pinkie not to be selfish and to leave some of the lollipop for *her*. Even though her daughter had been born prematurely at seven months old, by the time she'd turned two, she'd caught up to all the developmental milestones for her age bracket, and with her third birthday only a week away, she was actually ahead of where the pediatrician had predicted she'd be. She was talkative and bright, with an inquisitive nature and vivid imagination. And Katie couldn't imagine her life without Val's sweet innocence in it.

"Okay, I'm done," Katie announced once all the perishables had been taken care of. She only needed to deliver the gallon of milk and loaf of bread that she'd picked up for her neighbor and good friend, Avery, who was also Leah's mother.

"Yay!" Val squealed in excitement as she scooted off the chair, Pinkie Pie in one hand and the two lollipops in the other. "Let's go, Mommy!"

Val raced to the front room of the house, her dark brown braid bouncing off her back as she came to an abrupt halt in front of the screen door. She waited, shifting from sandal to sandal, her big blue eyes sparkling with anticipation for Katie to unlatch the lock. As soon as the door was open, Val bolted out to the front yard, then stopped at the sidewalk, just like Katie had taught her to do so she didn't run into the street.

They walked to the townhouse next to theirs, where Leah lived, and by the time Katie had reached their front porch, Val had already stood up on her tippy-toes to push the "ding-dong" button, as her daughter called it. The door flew open, with four-year-old Leah on the other side, who looked just like her mother, with auburn curls, freckles, and a cute button nose.

Leah clapped her hands together happily. "Val! You're here! I've been waiting and waiting and waiting!"

Avery came up behind her daughter and

rolled her eyes. "You'd think they haven't seen each other for weeks, instead of just hours," she said in amusement.

"I bwought you a lollipop!" Val said, thrusting it toward Leah while glancing back at Katie, her struggles pronouncing the letter "r" coming through. "Can we eat them now?"

Katie exchanged a mom look with Avery, and after being given the silent okay by her friend, she nodded. "Yes. Just remember that you have to lick it until it's gone, and don't bite into it."

"We know," the two little girls sing-songed at the same time, then ran off to Leah's playroom.

Katie stepped inside the house, indicating the items in her hands. "And for you, the bread and milk you requested from the grocery store."

Avery took the heavy jug from Katie's grasp and walked to the kitchen, where they could hear and see the girls playing through the video monitor set up on the wall. "Thank you. And for being such an awesome friend, you get the first piece of the coffee cake I just pulled out of the oven."

Katie inhaled the scent of cinnamon, sugar, and rich, buttery goodness. "God, it smells heavenly."

Avery put away the milk and set the bread on the counter. "Do you want coffee or iced tea to go with it?"

"Coffee, but I'll make it while you cut the coffee cake," she said, moving to the instant brewer and pulling out her favorite French vanilla pod to put into the machine. "Would you like one, too?"

"Yep. You know how I like it."

Yes, Katie did, because they'd shared many cups of coffee together over the years. After finding out that she was pregnant with Val, Katie had moved from her apartment in the city and purchased the small, affordable townhome in a more residential area. Avery, a stay-at-home mom, had already been living next door with her then infant daughter and handsome, doting husband, and the two of them had become immediate friends.

After Val had been born prematurely, it had been Avery who'd been there for Katie, supporting her emotionally and helping with the baby. Three months later, when her maternity leave with the ad agency she'd been employed by as a graphic designer had come to an end and she'd had to return to work, Avery had become Val's babysitter. But that childcare had only lasted six months, because Katie absolutely hated being away from her little girl for eight hours every day, and she never wanted Val to feel like she wasn't there for her—like Katie's parents had done. So, with the help of her boss at the ad agency, she'd started up a freelance business for graphic design, which enabled her to work from home. Best decision ever, as far as Katie was concerned, even if she had to budget carefully to make ends meet. Her daughter would always come first for her.

With two steaming mugs of coffee, with a splash of cream in each, Katie carried them to the kitchen table. She sat down just as Avery served her a slice of the coffee cake, then took the seat next to Katie. She moaned as the first bite melted in her mouth.

"I swear, you are the reason I can't lose the last ten pounds of my baby weight," Katie joked. "For over three years now, you've plied me with the most amazing cakes and cookies and sweets, and you know I can't resist."

"What are you talking about?" Avery said, dismissing the weight issue with a wave of her hand. "You look great . . . and there's a certain someone who's noticed what a hot momma you are with your fantastic breasts and curves."

Katie frowned as she took a sip of her coffee, unable to imagine who Avery was referring to. "Do I want to know who you're talking about?"

"Oh, my God!" her friend exclaimed, her expression and tone filled with exasperation. "Is your vagina that far into hibernation that it hasn't noticed or lusted after Garrett?"

"You mean the gardener guy?" she asked incredulously.

Avery huffed out a disbelieving laugh. "He's a great-looking *landscaper* who owns his own business, yet insists on taking care of your lawn instead of sending one of his minions to do the menial work. Trust me, that man is interested in more than pruning the bushes around your front porch."

Katie coughed, nearly choking on the piece of cake she'd been swallowing. "How the hell would you know this?"

A devious smile curved the corners of Avery's mouth as she set her cup back down on the table. "Because when I went out to check the mail the other day when he was mowing your lawn, he 'casually' asked me about you. I told him you were a single mom, that there was no father in the picture, and that you're way overdue to get laid."

"Avery!" Katie stared at her friend in horror.

"Okay, I didn't say the last part about you needing to get laid, even if it is the truth and you are way past due," she said, putting Katie somewhat at ease that her gardener wasn't privy to the lack of sex in her life. "But seriously, Katie, what would it hurt to go out on a date with him?"

Katie immediately shook her head. "I'm just not interested right now."

She hadn't gone out with a guy since Brice, and she didn't count her night with her fantasy man, Connor, as a "date." God, that seemed like forever ago, but she thought about him all the time . . . It was hard not to when her daughter's beautiful blue eyes were like a mirror of her father's.

"You have to start somewhere," Avery said, more softly now and with good intentions. "Don't you want to get married someday? Have a husband and more kids?"

Her stomach gave a pained twist. Now that was something she *didn't* like to think about. She already knew from her parents' experience that marriage wasn't all it was cracked up to be, and she never wanted to put one child through a custody battle and divorce, let alone a few more.

She finished the last bite of her cake and set her fork on her plate. "For right now, I'm good. I swear." She gave her friend a genuine smile. "I like it being just me and Val."

Much to Katie's relief, Avery let it go. While Katie finished her coffee and checked on the girls through the monitor, her friend took the dishes to the sink and washed them. Val and Leah were busy having a tea party with her dolls and stuffed animals, so Katie reached for the *Chicago Magazine* on the table, which focused on the city's politics, lifestyles, real estate, and culture. The glossy front cover featured the main spotlight for the month, "Chicago's Hottest Properties." Katie absently thumbed through the pages, checking out the advertisements like she always did. It gave her ideas for her graphic designs and kept her up to date on what kind of ads were most effective.

"So, is everything all planned for Val's birthday party next weekend?" Avery asked as she closed the dishwasher and dried her hands on a towel.

"Yep. I've got about twelve kids coming

from the Stepping Stone Academy, and their moms," she said of the preschool where Val and Leah went for a few hours in the morning, for socialization and developing cognitive skills, and so Katie had time to work uninterrupted. "The cupcakes and food will be delivered in the morning, along with the pink, girly bounce house. I even found a My Little Pony piñata that she's going to flip out over."

"Do you think she'll want to hit it with a baseball bat to break it open?" Avery asked with a laugh.

"She will as soon as she finds out there's candy inside," Katie said with a grin as she turned another page of the magazine, to the featured article, "Chicago's Hottest Properties."

"So true," Avery said as she put the rest of the coffee cake into a sealed container.

Katie skimmed through the article on the left-hand-side of the page, which lauded the city's most prominent real estate companies and builders—how they started out and why they were now multibillion-dollar businesses. It was an interesting piece, and once she was finished with the first page, her gaze skimmed over to the second one, where a new headline read, *One hot property, and one of Chicago's hottest bachelors!*

Beneath that caption was a picture of a guy standing next to a newly renovated home that he was obviously responsible for, located in a high-end neighborhood. Dressed in a dark blue T-shirt and faded jeans, he was leaning casually against a pillar, arms crossed over his muscular chest. She hadn't even looked at the man's face yet in the photo, but the tattoos on his arm riveted her gaze, not because of how intricate the ink was but how *familiar* those designs were, even three and a half years later.

The oxygen in the room seemed to evaporate as she forced herself to lift her gaze to his features to verify what her heart already knew. Her stomach bottomed out when she stared at those gorgeous blue eyes that had been at first so kind with her, then so hot and seductive. The charming smile on his lips seemed directed intimately at her, flooding her mind with a dozen different memories of their one night together before she'd snuck out of his room in the early hours of morning.

After all this time, she'd found him.

"Oh, my God." Her throat was so constricted that the words came out like a croak.

Avery strolled up beside her to see what had caught Katie's attention, her gaze landing on the magazine spread and Connor. "Oh, my God is right," Avery said a bit breathlessly. "What a freakin' stud."

"That's him," Katie rasped again, knowing she probably wasn't making any sense to her friend, but stringing more than two words together at the moment was proving to be difficult.

Avery gave her a peculiar look, her mouth quirking in amusement. "What, that's the guy you want to end your years of celibacy with?" she teased, then lowered her voice in deference to the girls in the next room. "Yeah, he's definitely fuckable. I'd do him, too, if I wasn't happily married."

Katie shook her head hard. "No," she said, finally finding her voice. "That's *Connor.*"

It took her friend a few extra seconds to process *who* Katie meant, and her eyes widened comically when it all became clear. "Connor as in . . . " Avery's gaze slid to the monitor and the dark-haired, blue-eyed little girl oblivious to the adult conversation about her *father.* "Holy shit."

Avery sank into the chair next to her, looking as stunned as Katie felt as the two of them fell silent. Her friend was the one and only person she'd ever told about her impulsive one-night stand in Denver that had ended in an unexpected pregnancy.

At the time, Katie had been beside herself because she literally had no information to contact Connor to let him know he was going to be a dad. Between the birth control implant in her arm and his condoms, never would she have believed a baby was possible. She'd even tried doing a Google search for "Connor Chicago Illinois," the only three things she knew about him—other than the fact that he'd given her the best sex and orgasms of her life— and quickly realized that Connor could have been his first or last name, which doubled the listings and references the Internet had supplied.

She'd been so overwhelmed, and knowing that locating her one-night stand was like trying to find the proverbial needle in a haystack, she'd resigned herself to being a single mom. And she'd been okay with that. While she'd never deliberately keep her pregnancy a secret from Connor, she'd be lying if she didn't admit that a part of her was relieved that she'd be raising her child on her own, because her greatest fear was that her daughter would be the one to suffer from a custody situation.

Her parents' marriage had been based solely on her mother getting pregnant, not on love, which led to a nasty divorce and a custody battle for Katie—not because either one of them really *wanted* her. No, it was to hurt the other person, and to use Katie as leverage for something they wanted. For her mother, it had been money and child support. For her father, it had been about keeping her so he *didn't* have to pay child support to the woman he'd come to despise. And for Katie, it had been about desperately trying to please both parents so they didn't keep tossing her back and forth to suit their whims.

The terrible memories were enough to make her stomach ache and anxiety to take hold, because she could no longer say that *she couldn't find Connor.* She'd found him, whether she liked it or not. And he deserved to know that he had a daughter. This wasn't about Katie and her feelings and fears. It was about Val, because Katie never wanted her daughter to one day resent her when she learned the truth, that her mother did know how to contact Connor but had instead kept Val's biological father from being a part of her life.

She glanced back down to the article, and

within the first few paragraphs, she knew more about him than she had minutes ago. All the pertinent information she needed to finally contact him was right there in front of her. She learned that Premier Realty was the business Connor Prescott co-owned with three partners. His role within the company was as a residential and commercial redeveloper who restored old homes and properties in the high-end areas of Chicago, then resold the real estate for a solid profit, and according to the writer, he'd done very well for himself in the market.

He was also being touted as rich, single, and available, with the magazine declaring him as being one of Chicago's hottest bachelors in the real estate industry. And judging by that flirtatious grin on his face that the camera had captured, he didn't seem to mind the title at all. He looked carefree, and like he was loving life as a bachelor.

Something in her chest tightened with a pang of disappointment. The night she'd met him, he'd claimed he didn't do one-night stands, but the fact was, Connor was a gorgeous guy who probably had his pick of women—no doubt more so now that *Chicago Magazine* had just made him a target for every woman out there looking to be the one to tame the hot, rich bachelor.

Not that any of that mattered to her, she told herself. But the lie was hard to swallow, because despite the fact that she'd snuck out on him that morning in Denver, there had been many, many times over the years that she'd wondered what if. What if she'd stayed in bed with Connor instead of quietly slipping out of the hotel suite? What if she'd taken the same flight home as him instead of rebooking on another airline to deliberately avoid him? What if they'd dated once they returned to Chicago? And the big one . . . what if she'd been able to tell Connor she was pregnant right when she'd found out? Where would they be now? Together? Apart? Battling over custody of Val?

That last thought caused her stomach to pitch again.

There was no way of knowing the answer to any of those questions, but what Connor didn't know was that she'd left him that morning because she'd felt too much for him emotionally. Beyond the mind-blowing and phenomenal sex, there had been a deeper connection between them from the moment he'd sat down at her table at the restaurant and he'd coaxed her humiliating story out of her, and the bond had grown stronger, and more intense, throughout the night. Every slow, sensual kiss, every erotic caress had elevated the intimacy between them. He'd been so selfless, her pleasure his sole focus—and oh, had he pleasured her, until her body had nothing left to give and her heart began to wonder about the possibilities with a man like Connor.

It had been those feelings that had scared her enough to make her bolt. At the time, she hadn't been at a place in her life where she was ready to dive into another relationship so quickly. Not on the heels of what had just happened with Brice, and all the other guys who'd come before him. She'd no longer trusted her judgment when it came to men, and still didn't, which was why being single and focusing on Val was all that mattered to her.

And now, she was staring at Connor, one of Chicago's hottest *bachelors*. And all the information she needed to contact him was just a matter of a few quick searches on Google.

The soft touch of Avery's hand on Katie's arm brought her back around. When she glanced up at her friend's face, she saw the worry and compassion directed her way.

"What are you going to do?" Avery asked, without any judgment.

Fate had finally decided to intervene, and now there was only one choice left for Katie, regardless of the apprehension and fears she was already battling.

"I'm going to call him and let him know he has a daughter."

BEYOND PISSED, CONNOR barged into Wes Sinclair's office without bothering to knock on the closed door—so it was his own damn fault that he found his business partner/brother-in-law making out with his wife, Natalie, who was also Connor's sister. Eight months pregnant, Natalie was sitting on Wes's lap, his hand just beneath the hem of her formfitting maternity dress while her fingers tangled in her husband's hair as the two locked lips. Hell, they didn't even stop at the interruption. No big surprise there. The two were insatiable.

"Jesus Christ!" Connor said irritably as he stalked up to Wes's desk, his surly mood increasing exponentially. "Don't you two ever stop?"

Very reluctantly, Wes ended the kiss with

his wife and smirked at Connor over Natalie's shoulder. "Yeah, occasionally. To sleep or eat. Sometimes to work. Although if you haven't noticed, it's currently *after* hours, so it's not like we're fooling around on the company clock."

As if that mattered, considering Wes co-owned the business with him and two of their other friends. "Yeah, well, you might want to give my sister a break. If *you* haven't noticed, she's about ready to give birth to my nephew, so should you really be doing all that . . . *stuff?*"

"Oh, my God, Connor," Natalie said with a laugh as she glanced his way, though she made no move to get up off Wes' lap. "Sex is perfectly fine while I'm pregnant, right up until I give birth."

"And pregnancy has made her horny as fuck," Wes just *had* to add. "So I'm just doing my part to keep her happy, which makes me an *awesome* husband."

Connor grimaced at the TMI. "*Stop.* You two are going to make my ears fucking bleed. We've had this conversation before," he said, more directed at his brother-in-law. "I do *not* want to hear these things about my sister, you asshole." It was just *wrong*, and he hated having to scrub those too-intimate images from his brain about his sibling.

Wes frowned at him and gently rubbed Natalie's substantial baby bump. "Hey, don't talk like that in front of my kid."

Connor rolled his eyes, forced to watch while his sister and Wes exchanged a more loving look before her husband pressed a kiss on her covered belly. Jesus. Connor never would have thought that a one-time player like Wes could settle down and become so domesticated. And with Connor's sister, no less, when at one time the two of them had been hard-core frenemies.

But it was hard to deny that they were ridiculously happy and that Wes was a devoted and one-hundred-percent committed husband— which was a damn good thing, too, because Connor had no desire to end up in jail for murdering his brother-in-law.

"Jesus, what's going on in here?" Max, their other friend and partner asked as he strolled into the office, too. "Well, other than Wes and Natalie messing around. Again," he added derisively.

Wes shrugged unapologetically. "Hey, the door was closed and Connor didn't bother to knock, so he should consider himself lucky that he didn't see more than he did."

Max nodded in agreement. "Good point, and it's so not fair that you have access to your wife since she works down the hall from you, while I have to actually go all day without seeing mine, unless we make a lunch date."

"Then why are you even here right now when it's nearly five thirty?" Wes asked. "Even Kyle beelines it home to Ella the second it's time to clock out for the day," he said of their fourth partner, who'd recently gotten hitched and his wife had announced that she was pregnant, too.

Connor was surrounded by domestic bliss on a daily basis, and in a few months, there would be a trio of newborns added to the mix and he'd have to listen to each one of them brag about their babies. All three of his friends had settled down and gotten married in the past year, and were soon-to-be family men and fathers, and Connor, still being single, was totally the odd man out. He'd never thought he'd be the last man standing when he *liked* being in a committed relationship . . . but he was still waiting for *the one* to cross his path.

Then again, there were days, and nights, when he couldn't help but feel that he'd let the one woman he'd wanted the most slip through his fingers. Or rather, she'd slipped out of his hotel room in the early morning, never to be heard from again. Yet three and a half years later and he still felt like he was hung up on Katie. Memories of her were the reason things hadn't worked out with the last woman he'd dated for a few months.

Hell, he still found himself looking twice at blonde women that were her height or had her similar features. She was *somewhere* in Chicago, and there was a part of him, albeit a stupid part, that wouldn't give up hope of finding her again.

He really needed to get the fuck over it, and her, and move on with his life. She'd probably moved on herself, and he was no doubt barely a blip in her memory bank.

"I was on my way out of the office to head home, too, when I heard Connor's raised voice in here," Max said, cutting into Connor's thoughts. "*That's* why I'm still here."

"Yeah, you did come in here a little high-strung," Wes added, goading Connor a bit more. "What's got your panties all in a twist anyway, Prescott?"

Connor's earlier resentment returned like a hot poker to his ass, and he glared at all three other occupants in the room. "Let me tell you exactly what's got my panties in a twist," he mocked in a sarcastic tone. "That fucking article in the *Chicago Magazine* that you all talked me into doing 'because it would be good exposure for the company,'" he said, adding exaggerated air quotes. "I didn't know I was going to be tagged as one of Chicago's hottest bachelors."

The corner of Max's lips twitched with humor, but Wes more blatantly laughed out loud, because they'd all seen the article and the featured spotlight that focused on Connor being a wealthy bachelor—and the two jerk-offs clearly thought his new celebrity status was funny.

He glanced at his sister, who blinked at him more innocently. He wasn't sure if pregnancy was genuinely making Natalie naïve or if she was just jerking him around in a subtler way. "Okay, so they might have taken some creative liberties with the article, but it *is* great exposure," she assured him sweetly, while her husband smirked from behind her. "The phones and client requests have definitely increased since the magazine came out a few days ago."

"So have *mine*, and not in the way I'd prefer," he said through gritted teeth, indicating the phone in his hand, which was ringing with an unlisted, unidentified number as he spoke. "Take my cell phone number and contact information off the goddamn website *tonight*," he said directly to Wes, who was tech savvy enough to get the job done. "I have women calling and propositioning me at all hours of the day and night since that article came out. Hell, I went to get my normal cup of coffee this morning at a place near the jobsite, and the barista wrote *her* name and number on my cup."

"Geez, you sound a little ungrateful," Wes drawled in a facetious tone. "Any other guy would be taking advantage of the surplus of women."

That wasn't his style. "These women are stalking me, and it's goddamn creepy."

"I'm sure it's not as bad as that," Natalie said, clearly trying to soothe him.

His cell phone beeped with yet *another* voice mail message, adding to all the other unwanted proposals, overtures, and indecent invitations from strange women. He decided to prove to his sister, Wes, and Max how *bad* it really was and show them just how shameless these women were in their approach.

"Since you all seem incredibly amused at my expense, take a listen to this last voice mail message so you can hear exactly what I've been dealing with." He opened his voice mail and played the last recording that had just come through, watching his friends' and sister's expressions.

"Hi, Connor," a woman's soft voice said, almost reluctantly, when he was used to far more enthusiasm from his recent female callers. "This is Katie Kaswell," she went on, and it was a name he hadn't heard of before. "I'm not sure if you remember me, but we spent the night together three and a half years ago during the snowstorm that shut down the Denver airport. I saw the article in *Chicago Magazine* and looked you up, and I was wondering if maybe you and I could meet up for a drink? You can call me at . . ."

She stated a series of numbers, but Connor's heart was pounding so freaking loudly that he couldn't hear any of it. Katie . . . *Kaswell.* After all this time, he finally knew her last name. And she wanted to meet up for a drink. Mind . . . fucking . . . blown.

Three pairs of eyes in the room stared at him in varying degrees of surprise (his sister), interest (Max), and hilarity (Wes, the asshole).

"Holy shit, Prescott!" his brother-in-law said enthusiastically, his gaze brimming with mirth. "Did you have a one-night stand in Denver after attending that conference on real estate investments well over three years ago?"

Connor's jaw clenched, and he didn't confirm or deny. He'd never told anyone about what had happened in Denver. For one thing, he wasn't the kind of guy who talked about his conquests. And for the second, he never thought he'd see Katie again.

Wes hooted in laughter. "Oh, my God, you totally did, you dog!"

Natalie smiled at Connor, softening her husband's more uncouth behavior. "I think it's kind of romantic that this Katie woman contacted you after all this time. You must have left quite an impression on her."

Connor had no idea what kind of impression he'd left Katie with, considering the abrupt way she'd ended their night together. In fact, his mind was still reeling over the fact that she'd contacted him. Now that she was just a phone call away, excitement mingled with an uncharacteristic bout of nerves and a heady sense of anticipation.

"So, are you going to call her back?" Max asked curiously.

"I think you should," Natalie urged supportively.

Wes surprisingly didn't have a smartass remark to make.

"Yeah, I'm going to call her back, but not in front of all of you." He didn't know what Katie wanted, but for what he had to say to her, he didn't require an audience.

That said, he left Wes's office and headed into the adjoining conference room, closing the door behind him. Then he dialed Katie's number and waited for her to answer.

Chapter Four

KATIE JUMPED IN her seat as her cell phone vibrated against the kitchen table, where she'd set it down just a few minutes ago. Her profound relief over Connor's voice mail picking up, instead of the man himself, was too short-lived, because the number that now lit up her screen was the exact same one she'd just called, leaving no doubt in her mind who was on the other end of the line.

She thought she'd have a longer reprieve to prepare herself for their reunion over the phone, but it wasn't meant to be. And considering she'd called him only minutes ago, there was no ignoring the call without it looking like blatant avoidance. Besides, Avery only had Val a little bit longer before it was time for her daughter to come home for the evening for her bath, then bedtime. The sooner Katie answered the phone, the sooner she could meet up with Connor, and the sooner she could get the inevitable conversation over with. *Ugh.*

Swallowing back the nerves gathering in her throat, she collected her composure and connected the call. "Hello?"

"*Katie.*"

Her name was a husky sound of disbelief that made her shiver, because it made her remember how sexy his voice had been when he'd murmured dirty things in her ear that night so long ago. *I bet your pussy tastes so damn sweet . . . Grab on to the headboard, Valentine, so I can fuck you long and hard . . . God, can you feel how deep my cock is, how desperate I am to fucking come inside you?*

"I'm having a hard time believing you called," he said, jerking her mind back to the present moment, though her cheeks remained warm from the seductive memories. "I honestly thought I'd never hear from you again."

He sounded . . . grateful, happy even, that she'd contacted him, and that was something she hadn't expected. "Well, I saw that article in the magazine, which led me to your contact information. I was hoping we could meet up somewhere and talk."

"Yeah, of course," he said, his tone enthusiastic. "I'd really like that. How about tonight?"

"Umm, nights are difficult for me." Which was the truth, since she had Val to take care of, though she was sure Avery would watch her if Katie asked. But meeting in daylight set a different and more casual tone, one that he couldn't misconstrue as a date. "Can you do lunch tomorrow, around eleven thirty? I live in Logan Square and there's a quiet café-type restaurant on Western Avenue called Charlie's that serves some really good sandwiches." She didn't ask him if he was familiar with the area. As a developer, he undoubtedly knew his way around Chicago.

"Okay," he said agreeably. "I can definitely make that work."

"Great." Before he could ask her anything personal, she did her best to end the call. "I, umm, need to go, so I'll see you tomorrow?"

"Absolutely. I'll be there." She heard the smile in his voice. "And Katie . . . I'm *really* glad you called."

She just hoped he felt the same way once he discovered he was a father to a three-year-old little girl.

✧ ✧ ✧

THE FOLLOWING MORNING passed at a snail's pace, even though Connor hit the ground running bright and early at six a.m. He'd already had a meeting with a professional demolition company to set up the leveling of a dilapidated home so new construction could begin on the piece of property Premier Realty had purchased in West Town, and another appointment with a city inspector for final approval on plumbing modifications made to an existing home they were renovating. He'd signed off on deliveries and scheduled various subcontractors on upcoming projects, and met with a few of the company's supervisors and his partner Kyle Coleman to talk about some safety issues.

And then it was *finally* time to head to Logan Square for lunch with Katie. He was wearing his normal, everyday work attire—a pair of jeans, a company T-shirt, and work boots—and he'd done his best to remain dirt and dust free. The drive to the café took twenty minutes, which made Connor ten minutes early. Wanting to make sure they got a table before the lunch rush arrived, he let the hostess seat him in a booth with him facing the entrance, and told the girl that he was expecting someone named Katie.

While he waited impatiently for her arrival, he checked out the menu to decide what he wanted for lunch, then cleared out all the voice mail messages from that morning that weren't either clients, suppliers, contractors, or other work-related business. Since last night, he'd already had over a dozen calls from women who'd managed to find his cell phone number before Wes could take it off the website, and now that it was gone, Connor hoped to God that the craziness ended.

With the last message deleted, he set his phone on the table and glanced back at the entrance just in time to see a blonde woman walk into the restaurant by herself. One look at the familiar face that had been imprinted on his brain for the past three years and seven months, and his pulse seemed to double its beat in wild anticipation. She spoke to the girl at the podium, then the hostess glanced his way and pointed toward the table where he was sitting. Katie headed in his direction, giving Connor time to look his fill of her ... from the silky blonde hair that had once fallen halfway down her back but was now cut to her shoulders in a soft, smooth style, to the features that seemed impossibly more beautiful than she'd been before.

It was mid-September and still warm out, and she was wearing a casual summery dress that skimmed the curves of her body that he knew intimately, and revealed those long, slender legs he still dreamed about having wrapped tight around his waist as he drove into all that softness between her thighs. God, one look at Katie, and his own body responded as though it had been waiting all this time just for her to come back into his life. The notion was insane but undeniable.

He lifted his gaze back to her face, and he couldn't say that she looked happy to see him in return. There was a tentative look in her eyes as she approached, and when she'd almost reached their table, he stood and gave her a genuine smile.

"Katie . . ." he said, taking her hand and leaning in to brush his lips across her cheek—a liberty he probably shouldn't have taken until he'd confirmed she was still single. For all he knew, she'd wanted to see him for business or real estate reasons, and not because they'd once shared such an intense, passionate connection.

"Hi, Connor," she replied as she pulled back, a more discreet smile on her own lips.

She scooted into the booth across from him and he returned to his side, unable to take his eyes off her. "You look great," he said—which was a huge understatement, he thought. There was something about her now that was so mature, lovely, and alluring, immediately drawing him in and holding him captive.

"Thank you," she said softly, modestly, though she didn't hesitate to check him out, as well. "You look amazing, too. That Chicago's Hottest Bachelor title certainly fits."

He winced, hating just how uncomfortable that label made him, along with all the attention that had come with it. "When our company agreed to do the article, I thought I was giving a standard interview about the business and the real estate market," he said in explanation. "I had no idea they were going to tie in 'one hot property' to me being single. But if it managed to put me back into contact with you, then it was all worth it."

Before she could reply, their waitress stopped at their table. "Are you two ready to order, or do you need more time to look at the menu?"

"I'm ready," Katie said, seemingly appreciating the interruption and all too eager to order and cut the idle chitchat. "I'll have the chicken Waldorf salad and an iced tea."

The server jotted down her selection and glanced at Connor.

"I'll have the roasted pork Cubano sandwich and an iced tea, as well," he said, handing both of their menus back to the girl.

Once she was gone, he returned his attention to Katie, all too aware of how uneasy she seemed with him, which he found odd. She'd been the one who'd called him to set up the lunch date, yet there was no misconstruing how guarded her demeanor currently was. Instead of leaning toward him in a more relaxed manner, her shoulders were straight against the booth cushion, as if she wanted to keep as much distance between them as possible.

It certainly wasn't the enthusiastic reunion he'd anticipated.

"So, how have you been?" He hated having to resort to small talk, but until he cracked that reserve of hers and was able to get her to warm up to him, polite conversation was all he had.

"Good," she replied, giving him nothing to go on. "Busy."

Ahhh, he jumped on that. "Busy" most likely meant work of some sort. "I don't even know what you do for a living," he prompted, just as their waitress delivered their iced teas.

A smile touched the corners of her mouth as she added two packets of sugar to her drink and stirred the tea with a long spoon. "I used to work for an ad agency as a graphic designer. Now, I'm self-employed. I work at home and do freelance jobs for different companies."

Silence again, and the longer it stretched between them, the more she started to fidget nervously.

"Are you seeing anyone?" he asked outright, because that would definitely clarify why she appeared so uncomfortable, but it certainly wouldn't explain why she'd sought him out after all this time.

Jesus, he was suddenly so fucking confused.

Her rich brown eyes widened in surprise at the question, and she shook her head. "No . . . I haven't dated since Brice."

Her confession took him aback, as did the pink coloring sweeping across her cheeks. Over three and a half years without dating? Just another bizarre twist to the entire situation, and something else for him to puzzle over, because it wasn't as if she seemed eager to date *him*.

So why the hell had she even contacted

him?

Their lunches arrived, and as she ate her salad, the awkwardness between them increased, as did her anxious demeanor. Any question he asked to strike up a conversation was met with a one- or two-word answer, and by the time they'd finished their meal, he was beyond frustrated by her strange behavior with him. The Katie sitting within reaching distance wasn't the one he'd spent the hottest, most emotionally satisfying night of his life with. No, his Valentine had been all soft smiles, breathy laughter, vulnerable sweetness, and openness and honesty, whereas this woman was tense and apprehensive.

He wiped his fingers on his napkin, set the cloth on his plate, and exhaled a deep breath to rid himself of the irritation building in his chest before expressing his disappointment. "Katie . . . I meant what I said when I told you I was glad you called, but I can't help but wonder why you even bothered to contact me when you act like you want to be anywhere but here with me."

She wouldn't look at him, her gaze on her half-finished salad as she toyed with her fork. "You're right, and I'm sorry."

He expected her to say she'd made a mistake, to get up and leave. What he never could have predicted was the fear in her eyes when she finally lifted her gaze to his.

She swallowed hard. "God, there's no easy way to tell you this . . . "

He frowned, because he couldn't imagine what had caused the dread he heard in her voice, and he was trying hard not to make assumptions—like, was she sick or something? "Tell me *what*, Katie? Whatever's wrong, I can handle it."

Her hands twisted together in her lap. "You have a daughter," she blurted out, her voice strained, as if she'd had to literally force the words out of her throat.

Her eyes were huge as she waited for his reaction, adding to his confusion. His brain tried to process what she'd just said, and how it pertained to him, but no matter how he rephrased her statement in his mind, he couldn't make sense of it.

He shook his head slowly. "I'm not sure what you're talking about. I don't have a daughter."

"Yes, you do," she said, her tone more insistent now. "Our night together . . . I ended up pregnant."

He stared at her in shock, feeling as though he'd just been blindsided. There was no misconstruing those words, yet he'd used protection and she'd mentioned that she was on birth control.

"How is that even possible?" he asked, still shell-shocked by the likelihood of a pregnancy happening when they'd taken twice the precautions—though his condoms *had* been in his overnight bag for over a year. "I could understand if there was an issue with one of the condoms, but you said you were on some kind of contraceptive."

"I was." She gave him a pained smile. "When I found out I was pregnant, my doctor looked up when I'd had my implant inserted. It had been three years, and while the device claims to last up to four years, with *up to* being the key words, clearly mine had failed early. And, I'm assuming, we also had an issue with one of the condoms we used."

He scrubbed a hand along his jaw, then braced his forearms on the table, not knowing what to say. To think that both forms of birth control had been ineffective was surreal . . . and holy shit, he had a daughter.

"She'll be three next weekend," Katie added.

Three years old . . . and then he frowned as he mentally did the math, and came up two months short on the timeline. "Are you sure I'm the father? If she's going to be three this month, that would have put you two months pregnant before we even met." Which meant that in all likelihood the child was Brice's, not his.

"She was born eight weeks premature at seven months," she said, bridging that gap of time as she reached into her purse for something. "If you want to have a paternity test done, I completely understand, but here's a picture of her for you to see."

Katie held a photo in her hand, and again, reluctantly—as if she really didn't want to show him—she turned it around for him to view. One look, and it was as though the breath was knocked from his lungs. She didn't look so much like him, but instead her delicate features were a replica of his sister, Natalie, when she'd been a little girl around that same age. But those big, blue eyes . . . yeah, those were all his, no paternity test needed.

The chubby-cheeked toddler was smiling

gregariously in the picture, sweetness and innocence with a glimpse of precociousness, and she stole his heart just *knowing* that she existed and was his.

"What's her name?" he asked around the lump that had formed in his throat.

"Her full name is Valentine, but everyone calls her Val for short."

He glanced up at Katie and smiled, because the name was absolutely perfect. "I like that."

"Considering the night she was conceived, she's been my little Valentine from the moment I found out I was pregnant." Their gazes held from across the table, and she shifted in her seat. "Connor . . . I want you to know that when I realized I was pregnant, I tried my best to find you on Google, but without a last name or phone number or any other personal information, it was impossible."

He nodded in understanding as he rubbed his thumb along the edge of the photo. "I get it." And he really did, though he wanted to say that if she hadn't snuck out on him, things might have ended up much differently. *He had a daughter.* And he'd already missed out on three years of her life. That knowledge hurt the most, because he never would have neglected a child had he known.

"I know that this has to be a shock, that you didn't expect to end up with a child after our night together." She visibly swallowed hard, her hands twisting in her lap again, though her chin lifted with fortitude. "And I want you to know that I don't need or expect anything from you. I'm not here for child support or to demand that you be a part of her life. I just thought you should know about her."

He sat back in his seat, unease curling through him as he studied Katie's determined expression. Even though she'd done the right thing by telling him about Val, there was no mistaking that she was deliberately downplaying his part as the child's dad and minimizing his responsibility.

Her emotional walls were sky high, and she claimed not to want anything from him, not even his presence in Val's life, but he couldn't say the same. Did she honestly think so little of him, that he'd be able to go back to his life the way it'd been seconds before? Before learning he had a kid? That he could erase this conversation from his mind and pretend he didn't have a little girl in the world? No. Fucking. Way.

She allowed him this time to think in needed silence, and he took it because his life had just been irrevocably changed, in ways he never would have imagined, but that didn't mean he couldn't figure out a way to adjust to whatever being a father entailed. Even if he was three years late.

There was no question he'd always thought he'd be married before he had a baby, that he'd be there for his child from the moment they'd been born, and that any kid of his would grow up with two loving parents, as he and Natalie had. This situation was far from the traditional ideals he'd envisioned for his future, but it didn't alter his core values as a man when it came to stepping up and doing the right thing for all parties involved.

Unless . . . He frowned. "Is there some other guy in your life that Val thinks is her father?" The thought of someone else taking on that role burned in his gut like acid.

"No," she said with a quick shake of her head. "I told you I haven't dated anyone since Brice."

Something didn't make sense to him. "Then why would you assume that I wouldn't want to be a part of Val's life?"

"Most men aren't prepared for an unplanned pregnancy or child. I'm just trying to be realistic." She shrugged, but the gesture came across as forced—she clearly wasn't as unemotional about these issues as she wanted him to believe.

"You're trying to be realistic?" He tipped his head, regarding her directly. "The *reality* is, we have a child together."

Her lips pursed ever so slightly. "Well, in my experience, having a child together and raising them in a co-parent situation isn't always best for the kid involved."

Ahhh, now they were getting somewhere. "In *your* experience? What do you know about co-parenting?"

She stiffened defensively. "Enough to know it's not always in the child's best interest."

Connor knew nothing about Katie's past, but his gut was screaming that the anxiety and fears he'd already glimpsed in her were based on something *she'd* gone through as a child, and her maternal instinct was to protect Val from the same pain. He couldn't fault Katie for trying to shield her daughter—*their* daughter—from any potential emotional fallout. He also understood that despite their one night together, she really didn't know him well enough yet to trust that he wouldn't be an unstable figure in the little girl's life. That would take time.

And even though he wanted to know what her *experience* had been, now was not the time. For the foreseeable future, all he could do was prove that he was rock solid and dependable when it came to the people in his life that he cared about. And whether Katie liked it or not, Connor cared not only about the daughter he hadn't met yet but about *her*, too.

He clasped his hands on the table in front of him, glanced from the sweet photo of Val still on the table facing him to Katie, and eased out a tight breath. "Just so we're clear, I had no idea when I woke up this morning that I'm the father of a three-year-old little girl. Will that take some getting used to when I've only known about her for, what, half an hour? Yes, I need to adjust to the realization that I'm a dad, but I'm not the kind of man who's going to shirk his responsibilities. If I have a kid, I will always be a part of their life, financially and emotionally and any other way that they need me."

"Okay," she said quietly, but he still heard the uncertainties in her voice.

Their waitress came by to clear their plates,

and after both he and Katie declined dessert, the server set the check on the table. He pulled it out of Katie's reach and placed his credit card on top of it, and was grateful when she didn't argue over the bill. What good was a shit ton of money if he couldn't buy the mother of his daughter a meal every once in a while, right?

He put his wallet back into his pocket, and there was one more thing he needed to address before they parted ways for the day. "I want to see her, Katie," he said gently. "I'm not looking to turn her life upside down or confuse her in any way, but she's my daughter and . . . " The rest of that sentence went without saying, and despite the misgivings in the depths of Katie's eyes, there was understanding there, too. "Can we start off with you introducing me as a friend, and go from there?"

He was asking nicely. Not demanding. There was no reason to make Katie any more skittish and worried than she already seemed to be.

"How about Sunday?" she suggested after a few long seconds had passed. "There's a private park right by where I live, and we can meet you there around eleven?"

Relief poured through him, and he quickly

accepted the offer. "That sounds great." He picked up the photo on the table. "Can I keep this picture? It would be nice to be able to show my family how adorable Valentine is." God, his parents and Natalie were going to flip out over the news when he told them he had a three-year-old daughter, though he had no doubt they'd embrace the little girl when they finally met her.

"Of course you can keep it," she said with a smile.

Once the check was taken care of, Connor walked outside with Katie. "Where's your car?" Wherever it was, he wanted to walk her to it, because now that it was just the two of them, without talk of Val as a buffer to their attraction, he was reluctant to let her go.

"I didn't bring one," she said, stopping on the sidewalk to look up at him. "I only live a few blocks away, and I walked here. It's a beautiful day, and I can use the sun and fresh air and exercise."

At the word *exercise*, his gaze automatically traveled down the length of her body in her pretty dress, taking in those perfect breasts he still dreamt about and the shapely dip and swell of her waist and hips that seemed . . . fuller now, curvier. His blood heated in his veins as the sensual memories of their time together in Denver jolted through him, and when he lifted his eyes back to her face, the flush on her cheeks told him that she was remembering, too. That the spark of chemistry and sexual tension was still there between them, even if she didn't want it to be.

"It's *really* good to see you," he murmured, and stepped toward her. When she didn't back up out of his reach, he took a chance and gave her a hug, gradually pulling her in close and wrapping his arms around her waist until they were pressed intimately together. She felt so damn good against his chest, and smelled even better. Soft and feminine and just like the Katie he'd spent Valentine's night with.

The Katie he'd never stopped wanting.

Her body was tense, and he stroked a hand down her spine, trying to soothe the fears he knew were there but didn't fully understand yet. "Just relax, Katie," he said, his mouth near her ear. "I swear I'm not the enemy or a bad guy or whatever else you think I am in this situation."

"I know," she whispered against his chest, but he wasn't sure he believed her.

But in time, she would come to understand

the kind of man he was, the type of father he would be to their daughter . . . and the relationship he wanted to have with her, as well.

Chapter Five

"KATIE, WOULD YOU stop pacing the kitchen?" Avery said, her tone exasperated. "I assure you, for the tenth time, you did the right thing."

Katie groaned in doubt, though she didn't stop her restless back-and-forth walk from the refrigerator to the sink, again and again. Since meeting with Connor for lunch a few days ago, a mountain of doubts had plagued her consistently and obsessively. Despite him trying to assure her that he wasn't a bad guy—which she knew was true after spending the night with him in Denver—she really had no idea what his intentions were as far as Val were concerned. And that uncertainty was a constant source of her anxiety.

Her horrible childhood and being in a tug-of-war between her mother and father on a consistent basis kept playing over and over in her mind. "What if he wants custody of Val?" she asked, keeping her voice low so her daughter, who was in the other room putting on her sandals, wouldn't hear.

Avery leaned her backside against the kitchen counter and raised a brow. "Connor is her father. Isn't that his right? He'll never get sole custody because you are an amazing mom, but any good dad would want part-time visitation rights of his kid."

Katie's stomach lurched, and she pressed a firm hand to her abdomen. "Do you think it's too late to move to another country with Val?" she asked, half-joking.

Avery caught Katie's shoulders as she passed by again, forcing her to stop and look her in the eyes. "You would never do that, and you know it. The fact that you told Connor about Val when you could have kept her a secret tells me what a decent, honorable person you are."

"What if that was a mistake?" she asked, praying that wasn't the case.

"I don't think it was, and deep in your heart,

you don't believe that, either. Give him a chance, Katie," Avery said, squeezing her arms reassuringly. "Until he does something to legitimately freak you out, give Connor this chance to get to know his daughter without thinking the worst or subconsciously sabotaging the relationship."

Katie drew a calming breath—actually, two of them for good measure. "Okay. You're right."

Avery grinned. "Of course I am."

"I'm weady for the park, Mommy!" Val announced as she came into the kitchen. She looked at Avery and frowned. "Why can't Leah go, too?"

"Because she's at home with her daddy today," Avery explained, since it was Sunday, which was her husband's day off to spend time with his wife and daughter.

Katie ran her fingers through Val's soft, fine hair in the back, which she'd left down for the day. Her daughter had insisted on wearing a green-striped headband with a bow, which didn't even come close to matching her pink polka-dot romper, but Katie was trying to raise an independent child, so as a mom she chose her battles wisely. Mismatched clothing and accessories were not the end of the world for a three-year-old.

"I'm taking you to the park to meet a friend of mine," Katie said, wanting to prep Val before they got there so her first face-to-face with Connor wouldn't be a complete surprise.

"Oh." Val's blue eyes brightened. "Is she my age?"

Katie held back a laugh. "No, my friend is a boy, and he's my age."

Val wrinkled her cute little nose in disappointment. "That doesn't sound like fun. Who is going to play with me on the jungle gym?"

Oh, the concerns of a toddler, Katie thought in amusement. "We'll figure that out when we get there, okay?"

"Okay. Let's go!" Val ran back into the front room.

Katie grabbed her daughter's My Little Pony backpack she'd filled with a snack and juice box for Val, along with handy wipes and sunscreen in case she needed to apply a second coat. Avery followed them to the door, then outside, and once they were on the sidewalk, they parted ways, with Katie and Val heading in the opposite direction to the park. Val insisted on wearing the backpack, which made her feel like a "big girl."

As they neared the small private park that was surrounded by a gate so only those in the community with a key card could use the facility, Katie saw a big white utility truck parked by the curb, which she knew was Connor's since she'd seen him get into the vehicle after their lunch the other day. He wasn't sitting behind the wheel, and after a quick glance around the perimeter of the area, she found him standing beneath a shady tree.

And God, he looked good. He was wearing a plain gray T-shirt and jeans, and though his attire was casual, his body still looked spectacular. His arms were big and strong, his shoulders wide, and even through his shirt there was no mistaking that everything about him was lean and trim. While he looked composed and collected, the closer she and Val got to him, the more she could detect subtle nuances of the nerves he was trying hard to keep concealed.

His thick dark hair, the same shade as Val's, was tousled around his head, as though he'd plowed his fingers through the strands several times while waiting for them to arrive. His hands were tucked into the front pockets of his jeans, and every few seconds, he'd shift from foot to foot. But it was the deep breaths she could see expanding his chest that told her he was struggling to keep calm in the wake of seeing his child for the first time.

"This way, sweetie," Katie said when her daughter started toward the gate leading to the park. "My friend is right over there."

Val followed close beside her, suddenly very shy, as she normally was around strangers, and especially men. As they neared Connor, he lifted a hand to acknowledge them, but he didn't start toward her or meet them halfway. Instead, he waited for Katie and Val to come to him, which she appreciated so he didn't startle or scare the little girl.

When they finally reached him, Val was clinging to Katie's leg and staring *way up* at Connor with huge, uncertain eyes. Connor swallowed hard as he lifted his own gorgeous blue gaze from Val to Katie. He smiled, but his expression was etched with awe that said, *Holy shit, that's my daughter.*

"Hi," he said, his voice a little rough around the edges with emotion.

"Hi," she replied softly in return before she gently touched her hand to the top of Val's head, who still hugged Katie's leg tightly.

"Sweetheart, this is my friend, Connor," she said in an encouraging tone, knowing it sometimes took a bit for her to warm up to newcomers. "Can you say hello to him?"

"No." Val shook her head stubbornly, a fierce frown pulling at her tiny brows. "I don't wanna."

Katie sent Connor an apologetic look, but before she could say anything else to prompt her daughter to be nice, Connor crouched down to Val's level so the little girl no longer had to crane her neck to look up at him. She still remained timid, but the grip on Katie's leg eased up slightly as Val eyed Connor more curiously now.

"You look very pretty today, Val," he said, his tone light and his smile friendly and approachable. "And you know what? Polka dots are my favorite, too. And that green bow in your hair is quite the fashion statement."

Katie had to swallow back a laugh at how sincere Connor sounded about her outfit, but his engaging comment worked like a charm with Val. Her daughter's blue eyes lit up at the compliment, and she let go of Katie's leg to touch her fingers to the material of her romper.

"I picked it all by myself!" she said proudly.

Connor looked unduly impressed. "You did a *great* job." His gentle smile still in place, he slowly reached out and lightly grasped her little hand in his much bigger one, the contrast of his long, strong fingers against her tiny ones pulling at Katie's heartstrings.

Surprisingly, Val didn't pull away. Instead, they stared at one another, as if silently communicating, and the moment seemed to stand still for Katie as she watched the two of them get acquainted in their own quiet way. The situation could have gone badly, with her daughter yanking her hand back and deciding she didn't like Connor at all, which would have been awkward and uncomfortable. But there was a patience to him that made Katie's throat grow tight and clearly put Val at ease. He didn't force or push the little girl to accept him . . . Instead he tried to let Val make her own decision about whether or not she was ready to let her guard down around him.

Her little girl had great instincts, because slowly, gradually, she gave him a bashful but approving smile.

Connor released her hand, as if knowing he'd been lucky to touch her for as long as he had without Val severing contact. "So, what do you say we go into the park so you can play and show me what a good climber you are?"

"I'm a weally *good* climber," she told him, jumping up and down in excitement. "I climb all the stairs without Mommy's help now!"

"Wow, you're a big girl," he said, straightening to his full height again, though now Val didn't seem intimidated by how tall and big he was.

Val hooked her little thumbs into the straps of her backpack as they strolled toward the gate to the park. "That's what my mommy says, too. That I'm a big girl."

Katie smiled. "And what else do I say?"

"To hold on to the wail when I climb the stairs so I don't twip," she said, bobbing her head to each word she spoke.

The corner of Connor's mouth twitched with a smile of his own as he glanced at Katie. "Would that be *rail* and *trip*?" he asked, trying to decipher some of Val's words.

"Yes. She speaks well for her age, but her *r*'s and *w*'s get mixed up a lot of the time, especially when she's excited."

"It's adorable," he mouthed to her, his eyes sparkling with delight, and it was like Katie was seeing her daughter for the first time through another person's eyes.

Val's speech *was* adorable, but being the mom, Katie heard it all the time and the cuteness of it had subsided. But Connor was living it all for the first time, and Katie found *him*, and his reactions to it all, incredibly sweet as well.

After swiping her key card in the reader, the large metal gate unlocked, and Connor held it open while she and Val walked into the well-landscaped play area. There were tables for picnics, covered areas for shade, and a few large recreation areas for different age groups. Katie, or rather Val, led them toward the playground for toddlers and the grown-ups followed a few steps behind.

"This is really nice," Connor commented, taking it all in.

Katie agreed. "The community is one of the reasons I bought a place in this area. It's a great neighborhood, but there's peace of mind in knowing that the park where all the kids play is secure, and not just anyone can easily get inside."

"There's Wobbie!" Val said in a high-pitched squeal, and the little boy in the distance who was also in her preschool class called her over. "Can I go play with him, Mommy? Please?

I pwomise to stay where you can see me!"

That was always the rule, though the playground for the youngest age group had been built in a way that was open and exposed from every angle. There were no hiding spots or places that Val couldn't be seen at all times.

"Yes, go ahead," Katie said, waving to Robbie's mom, who was sitting near the playground with another woman, both of whom seemed fascinated by the man she was with—probably because it was the first time she'd ever been *seen* with a man, not to mention a hot, gorgeous, sexy one.

Val dropped her backpack on the ground and ran to the play set that was reminiscent of a small-scale replica of the Swiss Family Treehouse, but minus the tree, and it was positioned low, and safely, to the ground. Katie scooped up her daughter's bag and sat down on a nearby bench that was close to where Val was playing, and Connor slid into the seat right next to her. Not so close it was inappropriate, but near enough that she could feel his body heat, and the heady scent of his cologne wreaked havoc with her feminine senses.

Connor watched Val for a few quiet moments before speaking. "I know I might be biased, but Katie... Val is so beautiful and bright and such a happy little girl."

Katie heard the hint of longing in his voice, that maybe he was thinking about all the years he'd missed out on that he could never get back. "You're very good with her," she said, wondering if he'd had practice with any other kids. "Do you have any nieces or nephews?"

He shook his head and gave her a quick grin. "No, not yet, but my sister, Natalie, is pregnant and due in about a month. She's having a boy. It's just her and me, sibling-wise, and she's the first one in the family to have a baby." His grin turned wry as he realized his mistake. "Well, she was until a few days ago, anyway. I kind of beat her to it by almost three years."

"Yeah... how did that go for you?" Katie asked, watching as Val chased Robbie to the steps leading to the three-foot kiddie slide, her daughter's sweet laughter pealing in the air. "Telling your family about Val, I mean?"

"Well... I can honestly say that everyone was shocked." He laughed lightly. "But I explained the situation, and how you and I met, and as soon as I showed everyone Val's picture, hearts melted. She looks just like my sister at that age, and my parents can't wait to meet her, and you, too."

Katie tried not to let any panic set in over the fact that she would now have to share Val not only with Connor but his family, as well. It had just been the two of them for so long, and selfishly, a part of her was afraid of that sharing process and what it would entail. Long weekends away for Val with her dad, and Katie sitting at home alone? Custody arrangements with Connor where the two of them created a bond that Katie wasn't a part of? Her fears were endless.

Connor stretched his arm across the back of the bench seat but didn't touch her, though the part of Katie that had been without a man's touch since their night together wished those fingers would brush along the back of her neck or slide into her hair . . .

"Katie . . ." He waited until their gazes met before he continued, softly and with care. "I know Val already has a set of grandparents that she probably has a great relationship with, and I don't want to take any of that away from her, but my mom and dad also want to be a part of her life as grandparents, too."

His assumption was like a knife in her chest,

because her mother and father had no interest in spending time with Katie, let alone doting on their only grandchild. "My parents have never even seen Val." It hurt to admit the words out loud.

A confused frown etched his brows. "What?" he asked, as if the notion was impossible for him to imagine.

She exhaled a sigh, returning her attention to her daughter. "I'm an only child, and I really haven't been close with either parent since I graduated from high school and moved here to Chicago for college. They're divorced," she said, her voice tight.

"I'm sorry," he murmured sympathetically.

She shrugged as if it didn't matter, though deep inside, the scars were there, and she knew they always would be. "They separated when I was four, and it was *not* an amicable split. As soon as I turned eighteen and they weren't legally responsible for me any longer, they both went off and did their own thing, as far away from each other as they could, and I didn't hear from them very often."

"Where are they now?" he asked.

She nearly moaned when his fingers *finally* slid against the back of her neck and beneath the short fall of her hair, his touch warm and tender, his fingers still as calloused as they'd been that night in Denver. The physical connection between them, as light as it was, made her heart beat faster, made her feel not so alone. But that light brush of his hand also made her body soften in places and ache in others, and dear God, she wanted to scoot closer and curl into him like a kitten.

She focused on the question he'd just asked about her parents' whereabouts. "My mom is living in London with a guy she met there a few years ago, and my dad . . . well, I'm not quite sure where he is right now since he's moved around a lot. I told them both about Val when I found out I was pregnant, but neither one has ever made an effort to see her."

"Jesus," he said, his voice low but harsh. "That's pretty shitty."

She laughed, though the sound lacked humor. "After the childhood I had, it doesn't surprise me one bit. My parents are pretty selfish people."

When she cast a quick glance at him, she saw the furrow of his brows, as if he was thinking about what she'd just said and wanted to ask about the less-than-perfect childhood she'd mentioned. "I don't expect anything from them, and that way I'm never disappointed," she said, hoping to detour those questions in his gaze.

It was the bubbly sound of Val's voice as she told Robbie to go down the slide with her that thankfully had Connor glancing away to look at his daughter. The glee that escaped Val as she glided down the short sloping surface made a smile tug at Connor's lips.

"So, you've raised Val all on your own, without any help from anyone?" he asked, his gaze still on his daughter.

"For the most part, yes," she said, knowing he meant close family. "My neighbor and good friend, Avery, and her husband, are always there for me if I need anything."

He tipped his head her way so she could see his serious expression. "It wouldn't have been that way had I known. You would have always had someone there for you and Val."

She believed him, that he would have been a father who was present in Val's life given the chance . . . and would be from here on out. "I'm sorry you missed out on the first three years of Val's life," she offered, meaning it.

"Me, too." The big, warm hand still at the

nape of her neck slowly moved, until his thumb stroked intimately along her jawline. Their gazes held, his filled with heat and desire and more questions she wasn't sure she wanted to answer. "About that night in Denver—"

"Mommy, can you push me on the swing?" Val asked as she came barreling up to Katie, defusing the moment between her and Connor and effectively deterring anything else he might have said or asked. "I want to go as high as the sky!"

Without missing a beat, Connor lowered his hand from her face and turned his full attention to Val. "What do you say I push you on the swing so your mom can sit and relax and enjoy the day?"

Val gave him a skeptical look, but Connor wasn't dissuaded.

Leaning toward Val, he bent his arm up and pointed to the taut bicep now bulging around the sleeve of his T-shirt. "See this big muscle right here?" he asked Val, and the little girl nodded, eyes wide as she stared at the impressive swell of sinew in his upper arm that made even Katie want to swoon. "That means I'm *super*-strong, and I can push you much higher than your mom can."

"Okay," Val agreed.

Katie rolled her eyes. A gorgeous guy flexing his muscles was all it took to convince Val to give in to him.

Her daughter ran off toward the swing set, and Connor stood, a pleased grin on his too-handsome face.

"Oh, my God," Katie said, pure amusement in her voice. "You're shameless, using your muscles to sway a girl like that."

He laughed, the sound low and intimate and, yes, completely and utterly *shameless* as he met her gaze. "It worked on her mom, didn't it?" he said, and with a sinful, sexy wink at her, he followed Val, a cocky strut in his walk.

She was suddenly feverishly hot, and it had nothing to do with the sun overhead. Yes, his magnificent body *had* made her weak in the knees, and there wasn't a night that went by that she didn't close her eyes and remember what it felt like to run her hands over his hard chest, those taut abs, those strong thighs . . .

Damn. She shifted on the bench and cut off that line of thought before she spontaneously combusted out in public.

She focused on Val and Connor instead, and the effortless way he picked her up—*with those big, muscled arms*—and helped her into the little bucket seat, designed so that younger children wouldn't fall off, or out of, the secure chair. He pushed her as promised, but clearly tempered his true strength so that Val didn't go *too* high. Her little girl giggled as the swing soared up into the air, her little legs kicking back and forth as she raised her arms to touch the sky.

After a good ten minutes, Val announced that she was thirsty, and Connor stopped the swing to let her down. They walked together toward Katie, with Connor still pouring on the charm.

"So what do you think, Val? Did my muscles work?"

Val nodded exuberantly, and lost in her enthusiasm, she looked up at Connor and slipped her tiny hand in his, already trusting him. "You *are* stronger than Mommy. I almost touched the clouds!"

Connor smiled down at her, and Katie could nearly see the lump in his throat that he had to swallow back because of the way his daughter had, without thought, just held his hand. "Next time, we'll try harder."

"Okay." Val beamed up at him, clearly already won over by her daddy, which Katie completely understood.

When the two of them reached the bench where Katie was still sitting, she already had Val's juice box out and the straw in it for her. Her daughter gulped down the apple juice and Connor sat down in the space next to her again, his thigh pressing lightly against hers.

The whole scene seemed so . . . normal. This was probably going to be their new routine for a while, she realized. Meeting up somewhere, being with Val together, and eventually, when the little girl was comfortable enough, Connor would take her for a few hours on their own, then maybe an entire day, then weekends . . .

"Want some of my juice?" she asked Connor, offering him the box she'd just drunk from as she leaned against his leg and nearly batted her lashes at him.

He gently touched her hair. "I'm good, but thank you."

She took another sip, then lifted her free hand and tried to show him the gesture for three fingers. "Did you know I'm going to be this many fingers on my buthday?"

The corner of his mouth twitched with a

grin at her attempt to hold her thumb and pinkie finger together. "Yes. Your mom told me that you're having a birthday soon."

"I am. With cupcakes and presents!" She did a little hop-skip on her feet in her excitement, then blinked up at him guilelessly. "Are you coming to my party?"

She saw Connor hesitate before saying, "That's up to your mom."

He didn't look Katie's way, and she realized that he was truly leaving the decision up to her, without any pressure. But he'd already missed two of Val's birthdays, and she wouldn't keep him from being a part of her third.

"Yes, of course he's invited to your party," she said, feeling yet another shift in this three-way dynamic where Connor was now a part of all those special events.

"Yippee!"

While Val hopped around like a human jumping bean, Connor finally looked at Katie, his eyes warm and grateful as he mouthed the words *thank you* to her.

Chapter Six

CONNOR LAY IN bed, one hand behind his head as he flipped through the channels on the TV mounted on the wall, trying to find something that interested him. At this point, he didn't think it mattered what show he watched, since his mind really wasn't able to concentrate on a program when he instead kept thinking about Katie.

It had been three days since their time together on Sunday at the playground, and while she'd agreed to invite him to Val's birthday party that upcoming Saturday afternoon, Connor knew he had to take things slow and steady with both girls. He didn't want to overwhelm either one of them by insisting he see Val every single day when he was still a stranger to the little girl, though that was definitely something he intended to build up to.

He also understood that after three years of being a single mom, Katie had a set routine with their daughter, and Connor was doing his best to be respectful of not making too many changes in the little girl's life too quickly. That kind of disruption wasn't fair to either Val or Katie, and for right now, he had to be content with the few things Katie had agreed to when it came to him forging a relationship with his daughter.

So, even though he didn't physically see Val every day, they did talk on the phone each evening at seven, right before her bath time and after he was home from work for the night. That was their deal, because it was important to Connor that Val at least heard his voice on a daily basis, so she'd remember him since he was going a whole week without seeing her until her birthday party. The next time they were face-to-face, he wanted her to be comfortable with him and not have to start from scratch all over again.

He loved their nightly conversations, anticipated them, actually. Val was so animated, so inquisitive, and such a chatterbox. When he asked about what she did that day, she had no problem telling him all the details of spending time with her mom or what had happened at her preschool or what she and her friend, Leah, had done. And somewhere along the way she'd picked up the phrase "catcha later" that she used with him at the end of their phone call, instead of saying good-bye. He liked that they were already establishing those special personal phrases between them.

When he called at the designated time, Katie always answered, but she quickly handed the phone to Val, telling him she was going to run the little girl's bath while they were talking—deliberately never giving them enough time to have a conversation of their own, which was starting to annoy him, because as much as he enjoyed his time on the phone with Val, he wanted to get to know Katie better, too.

He still felt something for her, the attraction between them was still strong, and now his emotions were involved. She was the mother of the child he was just getting to know, but she was also a woman he'd enjoyed spending time with in Denver. In fact, regardless of Val, he would have wanted to get to know Katie better and spend time with her again.

There was no doubt she had her guard up where he was concerned, and a part of him understood that she was trying to protect herself from being hurt in any way—clearly after Brice she had trust issues with the male gender. After hearing her story about her parents, he also knew her own father hadn't set a great example of showing his daughter how real men treated the women who were important to them in their lives or how a man should take care of his children.

So yeah, Connor definitely had his work cut out for him with Katie. Tearing down those defenses was his goal, and if he had to start with the physical attraction to build on the emotional trust, then so be it. He already knew by the few touches they'd shared that Katie was still interested in him physically, that given a little push in the right direction, she'd be as soft and sensual and uninhibited as she'd been with him in Denver.

He wanted that with her—a relationship that not only included Val but one that the two of them could gradually build upon when it came to all those subtle, sensual glances she gave him and the desire she tried hard to disguise but he was one hundred percent attuned to. And he had no issues taking advantage of that chemistry since it was definitely mutual.

He glanced at the time on his cell phone—9:20 p.m. He inserted his Bluetooth into his ear so he could be hands free and took a chance and called Katie. She answered on the third ring, her soft, husky voice washing over him like a warm, well-placed caress.

"Connor?" she said, clearly surprised to hear from him so late.

"Yeah, it's me," he replied, turning off the TV with the remote to give their conversation one hundred percent of his attention. "Did I wake you up?"

"No. I'm in bed reading. But Val is already asleep . . . unless it's important for you to talk to her?"

Of course she would assume his daughter was the reason he'd called. That's the way it had been for the past three days. "I didn't call for Val. I called to talk to you."

There was a distinct pause before she asked, "Is everything okay?"

"Everything is good, Katie," he assured her. "This call is strictly about you and me, and getting to know *you* better."

"Why?"

He sighed, hating the skepticism in her tone but not surprised, either. The men in her life previously had clearly fucked her over and Connor had to remind himself that patience with Katie was key. "For one, you're the mother of my kid, but make no mistake, that's not the only reason I want to know you better. You and I had something special that night in Denver and I think you still feel the chemistry, too."

"It was just sex, Connor." The words sounded forced, as if she was trying to convince herself of that fact. "A fantasy about having sex with a stranger in a hotel room, remember?"

He pushed his hand through his hair and clenched his jaw in frustration. Oh, yeah, he fucking remembered everything about that hot, erotic fantasy that had been so passionate and real, and he wasn't going to let her reduce their time together to something so meaningless, even to protect her own emotions, when he'd felt that connection between them.

"I'm going to have to call bullshit on that, sweetheart," he drawled, blatantly calling her out. "If it was just casual sex, then why did you leave in the morning without waking me up or saying good-bye? Why didn't you leave me your contact information? And why did you change your flight so you wouldn't have to see me?" All the questions he'd spent over three and a half years wondering finally came spilling out.

"Because I was in a bad place in my life and . . . I wasn't ready for another relationship when I couldn't seem to get it right with the guys I dated."

He heard the raw honesty in her voice and appreciated that she was at least giving him the truth. "And now?"

"Now I'm a single mom and I have a daughter I need to take care of," she said, her voice much softer.

Her walls were back up, her words meant to make sure Connor knew she had no room in her life for a man or a relationship—but he wasn't going to let her off so easy when it came to building something special between them. "What about *you*, Katie?" he asked, wanting to know that she mattered, too. "Who takes care of you?"

"I don't *need* a man," she replied firmly. "I can take care of myself."

"But wouldn't it be nice if you had one who took care of you every once in a while?"

She sighed, and he could feel her gradually

relaxing, those defenses dropping. "I'm not sure I know what that's like, and sometimes it's easier to just depend on yourself and not be disappointed . . . or hurt."

"It doesn't have to be that way. Some guys *like* taking care of their women."

"Mmm," was her undecipherable response.

She was so jaded, clearly based on all her own experiences. So, he decided to take a different approach with her, and while Connor knew he was taking a huge risk by going the sexual route with his next question, it would at least force her to think about what they'd had together back in Denver. What they could have again.

"Katie . . ." he said, invoking a teasing note to his voice. "I want you to tell me something . . . when you're alone at night, *taking care of yourself*, are the orgasms you give yourself as good as the ones *I* gave you?"

She sucked in a shocked breath, obviously not expecting him to be so bold and daring, but he wasn't going to tiptoe around their attraction. "All you have to do is give me an honest answer."

He half expected her to hang up on him, but then she laughed softly, dissolving the brief tension between them. "Truthfully, no." She exhaled a deep breath, as if gathering the courage to say more. "You're very talented when it comes to making a girl feel good."

"I *liked* making you feel good and I enjoyed taking care of you that way. I'd be happy to provide those orgasms anytime, Katie," he said, coaxing her along. "Want one now?"

He could have sworn he heard her breathing escalate. "It's late and we really shouldn't."

As far as protests went, it was a flimsy one, because she sounded like that was the answer she *should* say. Not the answer she wanted to give so she could feel good. So *he* could make her feel good. And there was enough excitement in her voice to tell him she liked the idea of him giving her that pleasure, and that's what he focused on for now.

Placing a hand behind his head, Connor stroked the other down his bare stomach to the waistband of his cotton shorts, his dick already perking up at the thought of trying out some dirty phone sex with Katie. "I won't keep you too long, sweetheart. I can have you coming pretty damn quick."

"That's quite a promise." Amusement and something more inviting mingled across the phone line.

She wasn't refusing him. In fact, now there was a bit of a tease in her voice, and he took advantage before anything changed. Like her mind. "Do you have one of those monitor things in your bedroom so you can keep an eye on Val?"

"Yes. Why?" she asked curiously.

"Because I want you to get up and close and lock your door, Katie," he ordered softly. "I'm about to make you feel so fucking good, and the last thing you want is our daughter walking in on you while your hand is between your legs and you're having an orgasm with me on the phone."

"God, Connor," she breathed huskily, clearly aroused by his explicit words.

"Take care of the door," he prompted again, and when he heard the rustling of the bed covers indicating that she'd gotten up, he took the time to strip off his shorts so he was completely naked, then settled on top of the covers.

A few seconds passed, and then she was back in her own bed. "It's done."

Ahhh, he had her, he thought, and breathed out a sigh of relief, and the eagerness in her voice made him grin. "Good girl. First things first. I need a good mental image. What are you wearing?"

"Umm, just a regular short nightgown and panties."

Immediately, images of the hotter-than-fuck underwear she'd worn on Valentine's Day popped into his head. "I don't suppose they're crotchless?" he asked hopefully.

She laughed. "No. Those are only for special occasions . . . I haven't worn them since you." She paused, then admitted, "I haven't been with anyone *since* you."

The realization that he'd been the very last man to fuck her was a heady rush. "Take your panties off," he ordered, taking his stiff cock in hand and wrapping his fingers tight around the girth. "I want to imagine you lying on your bed with your legs spread wide and nothing covering your gorgeous pussy." He gave her a few seconds to do as he asked, then said, "Before we get to that orgasm I promised you, you need to know that I have one huge regret about our night together."

"What's that?" she asked tentatively.

"For all the amazing ways that I fucked you, and all the times I made you come, there's one thing I never had the chance to experience," he said, his tone dropping seductively low.

"And what . . . what was that?"

Excitement made her voice unsteady, and listening to her getting turned on ramped up his own arousal. "I never had the chance to feel your mouth on my cock." Her soft little moan echoed in his ear. "It's a fantasy I've thought about endlessly since that night. Want to know how it plays out? And just to make sure you know what you're getting yourself into before you say yes, my go-to fantasy is hot and filthy and x-rated, and you, sweetheart, are so damn brazen in it when it comes to giving me what I want and need."

"*Yes.*"

One word had never sounded so sweet. Keeping a snug grip on his erection, he closed his eyes, picturing the erotic scenario in his mind, the one that made him come long and hard whenever he conjured it up. "It starts out with you and me kissing like we can't get enough of each other. Hot, deep, wild kisses that make me hard as steel. I'm leaning back against a wall, you're in front of me, and your hands are frantically trying to get my jeans open. You're so eager I have to help you, and once my pants are pushed down to my thighs, your soft hand is wrapped so tight around my dick, and you're already jerking me off, but I stop you because that's not how I want to come."

"How . . . how do you want to . . . come?"

Considering the choppiness of her sentence, he was pretty sure her own hand was busy between her legs. "I want to come in your mouth," he murmured, his stomach muscles tightening as a bead of moisture formed on the head of his shaft and he used his thumb to rub that silky fluid over and around the plump crown. "You want that, too, don't you, Katie?"

"Yes," she groaned.

"Yeah, I knew you would." His erection pulsed relentlessly in his hand as he pumped it slow and steady. "I push you down to your knees, and you go willingly, and when you look up at me with those dark brown eyes filled with lust, I go a little crazy. I fist my hand tight in your hair so I'm in control, and guide you toward me as I push my aching cock past your eager, parted lips. And fuck, your tongue is so soft, your mouth so damn hot and perfect, I know it isn't going to take much to make me blow."

She was breathing hard now, soft little unmistakable gasps of arousal, and it spurred him on.

He stroked his cock a little tighter, a little faster, feeling his climax building. "You have a mouth made in goddamn heaven," he said on a low, raspy growl. "And when I demand you suck me harder and deeper, you don't hesitate to obey. You accept every single inch of my dick, all the way to the back of your throat, and Jesus Christ, when I'm buried there to the hilt, you swallow around me, once, twice, and *fuck . . .*" *He was going to come.*

"Oh, God . . . *Connor.*"

He heard her inhale a sharp breath, heard her moan of pleasure escalate into a soft, muffled cry, and knew she was in the throes of her own climax. The tight pressure in his balls throbbed up along his shaft as his hips jerked upward and he pumped his erection through his fist, again and again. His orgasm erupted through him, the muscles along his abdomen clenching as his intense release nearly incapacitated him.

After they'd both had sufficient time to recover, he checked in on her. "Katie?" he asked in a gravelly whisper.

"Mmm?" She sounded sated and content.

He envisioned her relaxed on her bed, a satisfied smile on her beautiful face and her skin flushed as she enjoyed the orgasmic endorphins still ebbing through her body. "Is your hand still between your legs?"

"Maybe," she murmured huskily, the sexy, flirty lilt to her voice telling him which way that maybe was leaning. *Yes.*

He chuckled, adoring this lighter, more playful side to her that he'd missed—and wanted more of. "Did that orgasm make your pussy nice and slick with your release?"

Her soft exhale tickled his ear through the phone line. "Yes."

He took the fact that she wasn't trying to dissuade his dirty talk as a good sign. "I want you to do something for me, baby," he cajoled seductively, wondering just how daring she would be with him. "Taste yourself, Katie."

She was silent for a good fifteen seconds, probably in shock, before she responded in an uncertain tone. "Connor . . . "

"You just made yourself come with me on the phone, so don't go all shy on me now, sweetheart," he said, half-amused and the other half not letting her off so easy. "Put your wet fingers in your mouth and suck them. Use your tongue to get them nice and clean and imagine it's me licking the taste of your orgasm off of your fingers."

She made a soft, provocative "mmm" noise in the back of her throat that made him hard all over again. "That was so . . . "

"Fucking hot?" he finished for her, and she laughed. "The only thing that would make it any hotter was if I were there watching you do it in person, instead of imagining it over the phone. You're going to do that for me when I can watch, Katie. Very, very soon."

"You sound awfully confident."

Oh, he was. It was too bad she couldn't see his self-assured grin, because after tonight, there was no doubt in his mind that seducing this woman was going to be much more pleasurable than he'd imagined.

"And that very enthusiastic orgasm you just enjoyed?" he pointed out. "There's more where that came from," he promised, just to give her something to think about when he wasn't around. "Sweet dreams, Katie. I'll talk to you tomorrow night."

He disconnected the call before she could say anything more.

Chapter Seven

"SO, WHAT'S GOING on with you and your baby daddy?"

Katie glanced at Avery from where she was standing on a chair as she and her friend put up pink streamers across the patio's awning for Val's birthday party later that afternoon. Avery had come over to help with the decorations while her husband watched Leah and Val and put them down for a nap before all the activities began. Not only did it help not having any little ones underfoot while she prepped for the party and the bouncy house was being set up, Katie wanted Val to come home and be surprised to see the backyard transformed into a magical wonderland for her big day.

"My baby daddy?" she repeated in amusement as she stepped down from the chair and repositioned it in another corner.

Avery shrugged as she handed Katie the roll of crepe paper. "That's what he is. He's not your boyfriend. He's not your husband. He's the hot guy you hooked up with that resulted in a baby. So yeah, your baby daddy. How are things going with him?"

She hadn't had the chance to really talk to Avery since Katie had met up with Connor at the park the previous weekend. Between getting last-minute things ready for her daughter's party and being on a tight deadline for a few client ads that had claimed all her free time, she and her friend hadn't had any time to chat and catch up on things.

So, how did Katie explain how things were going with Connor when so much had changed in a short period of time? In the week since he'd met Val, Connor had talked to her every single night, and now her daughter expected Katie's cell phone to ring right before her bath time. The little girl carried the phone around with her, and as soon as it lit up and Connor's name showed on the display—which Val had already come to recognize—she'd run to Katie for her to unlock the screen and answer it first.

It was the sweetest, cutest thing to watch Val walk through the house talking to him—her daughter couldn't sit still—and how enthusiastic her conversation always was. She told him about her day, in more detail than Connor probably cared to hear, but there was no shortage of chitchat from Val.

Connor never talked to Katie right then. No, he always waited two hours later, when he knew Val was fast asleep at night, and then he'd call back so it was just the two of them on the phone. And just like her daughter, Katie had come to anticipate those calls, which always started out casually, with Connor asking about her day, or they'd talk about her work, or his business and his close friends, and his own childhood and family—which was the complete opposite of how hers had been, especially with his parents still being happily married.

There was a lot of getting-to-know-you stuff during the first part of their conversations, but somehow, someway, he'd inevitably say something that turned things hot and sexual. The man was a master at dirty talk—and no, she wasn't complaining—and for the past three nights, since that first phone call, she'd hung up the phone with her body relaxed and satisfied from the orgasm he'd effortlessly coax from her as his deep, husky voice filled her head with all the erotic, sinful things he claimed he wanted to do to her. Just remembering last night's panty-melting exchange made her face feel warm and flushed.

"Hello?" Avery snapped her fingers a few times, startling Katie out of her intimate and arousing thoughts. "Where did you go? You totally zoned out on me . . . " And then Avery's eyes grew wide in playful accusation. "Oh, my God! Have you and Connor been hooking up?"

"No!" Katie protested immediately, and threw the roll of streamers at her friend's head, hoping to distract Avery from her line of questioning—and anyway, phone sex did *not* equal hooking up.

Avery caught the bundle of crepe paper before it fell to the floor and completely unraveled, but her face was lit up with glee, like she'd just figured out a huge secret. "You're blushing furiously, Katie Kaswell, which I've never seen before. You and that hot hunk of a man are totally doing *something*."

Trying to ignore Avery, Katie stepped down from the chair. Finished with the streamers, she opened the package for the My Little Pony plastic tablecloth and started arranging it over one of the long folding tables that would hold the sandwiches and snacks.

Avery helped straighten the tablecloth, though her grin never wavered. "You know, it's okay to have a sex life even though you have a kid. You know that, right? You obviously had some kind of chemistry with Connor in the first place, so clearly the two of you are attracted to one another."

Yeah, desiring Connor and wanting him grew stronger every night when he seduced her mind and body. Katie didn't have many good friends, and she suddenly had the urge to talk to someone, to help her sort out all the confusing feelings swirling inside of her. Avery was her person, the one she trusted the most, and Katie knew her friend wouldn't judge her.

Katie arranged the matching plates, napkins, and paper cups on the table. "Connor has been talking to Val every day, which she loves and looks forward to. It's a great way for the two of them to get to know each other without it being forced. But later at night"—she met Avery's curious gaze, feeling her complexion warm all over again—"well, he calls me and we talk . . . and do things."

Avery laughed. "Do things? As in, phone sex?"

Katie nodded. "Yeah."

"Is it *good* phone sex?"

"*So* good," she admitted with a grin.

The man had a filthy mouth and a wicked imagination, which made the orgasms he enticed from her beyond amazing. While having phone sex was *safe* emotionally and physically, she'd be lying if she didn't admit that she missed *real* sex. The kind she'd had with Connor in Denver. Feeling his big, strong hands on her body, his mouth driving her wild before he pinned her down on the mattress and filled her with deep, driving thrusts that had her gasping with pleasure and need. Self-induced releases and vibrators just didn't compare to that, to *him*.

"So, you two have great phone sex," Avery said, pointing out the obvious. "Seems like a natural transition to doing it in person, don't you think?"

That was a question she'd struggled with herself. "I think Connor has every right to be a dad to Val, in every way, but I'm just not ready to be in any kind of relationship. With *any* guy."

Bottom line for her, she didn't trust her man-instincts any longer, and it was so much easier, and less complicated, with it just being her and Val. Then there was that fear of falling hard for Connor and getting hurt in the end when or if things didn't work out between them, because there certainly weren't any guarantees. She also had to remind herself that his picture had just been splashed all over a major magazine as one of Chicago's hottest bachelors, and he was probably a very hot commodity at the moment—although he did spend his nights with *her* on the phone.

"I'm not sure I get what the problem is," Avery said, bringing her back around. "Has he asked you to be in a relationship?"

Katie fussed with the pink and white balloons tied to one of the patio's pillars. "Well . . . no."

"Okay, so there's one fear you don't have to worry about, so why not just go for it and enjoy the sex? You already know how good it is with Connor, and it's not like he's a stranger. If you think about it, it's the perfect arrangement."

Over the past few days, Katie had surprisingly found herself coming around to that way of thinking. Considering all the things they'd already done on the phone together, it wasn't a stretch for them to transition all that sexual tension to a physical affair. They were clearly heading in that direction.

Luckily, Katie was saved from having to reply to Avery as the doorbell rang, which was the beginning of the various deliveries she had ordered for some of the food and the cupcakes. The bouncy house was finished being set up, and Katie put Avery in charge of getting the snacks in bowls and mixing the punch for the kids while Katie put together some party games for the little ones to play.

A half an hour before the event was set to start, Avery went back home to gather up the girls to bring them over so Val could be the first to see all the party decorations before her guests arrived. Katie took the short but free time to change into a comfortable dress, and just as she finished zipping it up in the back and slipped into a pair of sandals, the doorbell rang again.

Thinking it was Val and wanting to witness her expression when she saw all the party decorations for the first time, Katie rushed to the door and opened it without looking in the peephole. Seeing Connor standing on the front porch instead, looking so breathtakingly gorgeous, with his blue eyes sparkling with a genuine happiness and his sinful mouth curving with a smile . . . all that hotness nearly short-circuited her brain. It definitely had her body doing inappropriate things right before her daughter's birthday party.

"You're early!" she blurted out.

He tipped his head curiously. "Is that a problem?"

"I, uh, no . . . of course not." *Jesus, what was wrong with her?* "I just wasn't expecting you to be the first one to arrive."

His smile deepened. "I wanted to see and talk to Val before the party starts and her attention becomes all about the games and presents and cake."

"Oh. She's not here yet." She nervously smoothed a hand down the front of her dress. "She stayed over at my neighbors for the afternoon while I got everything ready for the party so it would be a surprise when she saw it. She should be here soon."

"Okay . . . " His brows rose, his eyes now glimmering with humor as she continued to stare at him. "Can I come in?"

Oh, my God. Get it together, Katie! "Yes, of course!" She stepped back as he walked inside, and she noticed for the first time that his hands were filled with numerous gift bags that were clearly for a little girl's birthday party. "You've got at least a half dozen presents. How badly did you spoil Val?"

"I swear I didn't go overboard," he promised. "And these aren't all from me."

That surprised her. "Oh?"

"A few of them are from my sister and my parents."

Why that made her feel . . . bad, she didn't know. Considering her own parents had never even met Val, she never expected his family to accept the little girl so easily without ever meeting her. "I'm sorry they weren't invited," she said, meaning it. "I . . . just didn't want Val to be confused by seeing people she didn't know or recognize on her birthday."

"They understand the situation, Katie," he said, not at all offended. "My mom and sister were just excited to buy some girly stuff and toys. I couldn't very well tell them no. They'll meet Val soon enough."

He set all the bags on the coffee table in the living room and then turned back toward her. "I have to say, this has been one of the longest weeks of my life, but my phone calls with Val have gone a long way in keeping me from getting too impatient," he admitted, right before his eyes went a little darker and more intimate. "And our phone calls . . . well, those kept me pretty damn happy, too."

His gaze dropped to her lips, which she'd just dampened with her tongue, and when he stepped closer, she didn't move back, because the desire flaring to life inside of her kept her riveted, and dear God, she wanted him to kiss her. Ached for the feel of his lips sliding against hers . . . not the fantasies he spun on the phone, but with the flesh-and-blood man.

Blinking slowly, sensually, he lifted a hand toward her face, and as his fingers touched her jaw, Katie heard her daughter's high-pitched voice from the front yard outside, heading toward the door. That snapped her out of her trance, and she jerked back just as the door burst open and her daughter ran through, wearing the cute pink party dress that Katie had given Avery to change Val into, and her hair pulled back into a ponytail with a pink bow.

Val came to a sudden stop when she saw Connor, the little girl's eyes slightly narrowed and confused, and Katie could nearly feel the anxiety pouring off of Connor, that his daughter wouldn't remember who he was since she hadn't seen him since last Sunday.

"Happy birthday, Val," he finally said, and it was the rich timbre of his voice, which his daughter had heard every single night, that made a huge smile spread across her face and light up those matching blue eyes.

"Connor!" she said happily, clasping her hands beneath her chin. "You came for my buthday!"

"I said I would." He smiled at his daughter, the softness in his eyes making Katie's heart swell with a startling emotion.

Val's eyes widened as she caught sight of all the gift bags on the table. "Are those for *me*?"

"Yes," he said with a light laugh at Val's enthusiasm. "But first, I think your mom has something to show you for your birthday."

Val ran over to Katie and tugged on the skirt of her dress. "Show me, Mommy! Show me now!"

Katie touched the top of Val's bouncing head. "In just one minute," she said before glancing back at the two grown-ups in the living room.

While Connor's attention had been focused solely on Val, Avery had been blatantly checking out her *baby daddy*. Her friend had seen the picture of him in *Chicago Magazine*, but Katie knew that eyeing Connor live and in person was far more impactful and magnified his good looks, personality, and charm by tenfold.

"Connor, this is Avery, my good friend and neighbor," Katie said, introducing the two of them. "And that adorable little girl is her daughter, Leah."

He gave them an amicable smile that only made him more breathtakingly handsome. "Nice to meet you both."

"Likewise," Avery said, completely enamored of him.

Katie held back, just barely, from rolling her eyes at her *married* friend.

"Show me, Mommy!" Val said exuberantly, reminding Katie of what awaited her daughter in the backyard. "Show me, now, pwetty please!"

"Okay, come on." Katie took Val's hand and the five of them headed toward the back of the house.

Val swung Katie's arm back and forth as they walked. "I've been waiting and waiting all day long for my party and . . . "

Her daughter's squeal of delight cut off whatever she'd been about to say as they stepped out to the patio and Val saw all the streamers, balloons, and the My Little Pony piñata and other decorations that had transformed the backyard. There were cupcakes and goodie bags for the kids and fun games set up out on the lawn, along with the big, pink bouncy house that looked more like a castle for a princess.

"Is this for *me*?" Val asked in awe.

"Yes, baby, it's for you," Katie said. It was the first time she'd really gone all out for her daughter's birthday, and seeing her guileless reaction, she was glad she had.

Val went up to Connor and slid her hand into his, as if it were the most natural thing in the world for her to do. "I want to go in the big castle," she said, giving him a hopeful smile. "Will you take me?"

"Me, too!" Leah said, grabbing his other hand because she didn't want to be left out of the fun.

Connor laughed, surprisingly comfortable being the object of both little girls' attention—whereas some men might not be as tolerant. "Come on, I'll go with *both* of you," he said, clearly not wanting either one of them to feel ignored or that he was playing favorites.

The trio headed toward the bouncy house,

with Katie and Avery watching them go.

"Oh, damn, girl," Avery said on a wistful sigh. "Your baby daddy is *so* fine. And the way he is with Val ... I swear my ovaries just exploded."

Katie gave her friend an incredulous look at her outrageous comment. "Seriously?"

"Oh, yeah. Mark my words. There are going to be a few single moms here today who you are going to have to beat off with a stick."

Katie shook her head. "I'm not his keeper, Avery."

"You should be," her friend said with a sly smile. "Even if it's just to keep him as your baby daddy with benefits."

Katie declined to respond to that remark. She and Connor shared a child, and despite their phone sex sessions, the truth was they weren't in a committed relationship, and he *was* free to date other women.

Except that mental pep talk came to bite her in the ass a few hours later, when the party was in full swing and the moms who'd elected to stay during the festivities zeroed in on Connor, who was the only guy at the party. Even Avery's husband had opted to stay home and watch football over being around a dozen screaming, sugar-fueled kids with endless energy to burn.

Katie had introduced him as a friend when everyone arrived, because until Val knew that Connor was her father, she didn't want her daughter to hear the information secondhand somewhere else. But delegating Connor to the friend zone for the day did have a few of the single women eyeing him with too much interest while he spent most of his time playing with the kids out on the lawn and around the bounce house. The little boys climbed all over him like he was their own personal jungle gym, while the girls demanded his attention, too, and Connor did his best to keep them all happy while looking like he was actually *enjoying* himself.

Julia, a recent divorcee, strolled up to where Katie and Avery were cleaning up the paper plates, napkins, and cups scattered on the table now that the kids were done eating. The other woman was in her late twenties, with long, bleached-blonde hair. Her petite height was out of proportion to her huge, fake boobs, and she never failed have her figure on display. Today she was wearing a formfitting camisole that displayed an ample amount of cleavage, a pair of cute lacy shorts that showed off her tanned legs, and four-inch wedge heels.

"Your friend looks very familiar," Julia said, talking as Katie kept clearing away the trash so she didn't have to do it all when everyone left. "But I can't place where I've seen him before."

"I thought the same thing," another woman, Rachel, said, adding her input to the conversation. "I keep thinking he's that guy who's featured in this month's *Chicago Magazine* as Chicago's Hottest Bachelor. The property redeveloper. Is that him, Katie?"

From across the table she and Avery were still clearing, her friend gave Katie an unmistakable look that said, *You better claim him, and quick, and shut those bitches down.* Except she wasn't going to publicly claim Connor, and she wasn't going to lie to Rachel and Julia, either.

"Yes, that's him," she admitted.

Avery groaned beneath her breath and shook her head in disappointment.

"My God." Julia's interest perked up even more as she gazed out at Connor with newfound enthusiasm. "Single, drop-dead gorgeous, and probably rich since he's part owner in a real estate business. And he seems to love kids."

Rachel laughed. "Sounds like you're already sizing him up as husband number two."

"Oh, he definitely has potential." Julia studied Connor a few seconds longer before a slow smile curved her overly plump lips. "You know, he looks hot and thirsty. I think I'll take him a cold bottle of water and save him from all those annoyingly hyper kids. Think that'll earn me a date?"

"It's worth a try," Rachel said, encouraging the other woman since she herself was already married.

Julia grabbed a bottle of water from the cooler and made her way out onto the lawn, which wasn't an easy feat in four-inch wedges. But she was clearly determined to be a good Samaritan and make sure that Connor stayed hydrated. When she reached where he was, she shooed away the little kids he was playing ball with and handed him the cold water.

Katie tormented herself by watching the exchange between the two of them. She couldn't hear their conversation, but she could see Connor's charming smile, as well as the way Julia laughed at something he said, then flipped her hair over her shoulder while making sure her chest was pushed out in a way that Connor couldn't easily overlook.

Ugh. Katie hated the slow burn of jealousy

that coursed through her, which only increased in temperature when Julia grabbed Connor's arm to look at his tattoos. She brazenly ran her fingers over the ink, her smile undeniably flirtatious, but the kicker came when the other woman pulled her phone from the back pocket of her shorts and began typing something into it. The only thing Katie could think was that she was exchanging numbers with Connor.

Katie threw away the last of the ripped wrapping paper from the presents Val had torn open a little while ago, her stomach in an uncomfortable knot. And it didn't help matters when she glanced at Connor and Julia again and found him looking at *her* while the woman in front of him had her head down as she continued to do something with her phone.

His speculation only made her feel self-conscious, and after gathering a few bowls and empty platters, she carried them into the house and sequestered herself in the kitchen so she didn't have to witness her *baby daddy* making a date with Julia. For the next fifteen minutes or so, she made herself busy putting away leftovers and washing the dishes, knowing that Avery had everything covered out in the backyard.

Finally, when she couldn't hide out in the

house any longer since she had guests outside, she exhaled a deep breath and prepared herself to deal with whatever Julia and Connor were currently doing together.

She turned around from the sink, a startled gasp escaping her when she saw Connor leaning oh-so-casually against the doorframe that led into the kitchen. His arms were crossed over his broad chest, his expression concerned. She hadn't heard anyone come into the house, and she had no idea how long he'd been standing there, watching her.

The thought was unnerving. "I was just getting some cleaning done so it doesn't take me hours to do when everyone is gone," she said, in case he'd come to find out where she was and why she'd been missing. The last thing she wanted him to think was that she was battling a green-eyed monster.

His gaze searched her face, his eyes too perceptive. "Are you okay?"

"Of course," she said, realizing too late that she'd jutted her chin out much too defensively. "I'm fine. Why do you ask?"

He pushed away from the doorway and slowly approached her, making her heart race with each step he took in her direction. "Because I saw the way you were watching me and Julia before you came in the house, and you didn't look fine."

Somehow, she managed a nonchalant shrug and glanced toward the floor and away from those intense blue eyes. "It's none of my business what you do with other women."

He touched his fingers to her chin and forced her gaze back up to his, his thumb brushing along her bottom lip. "Do you honestly think that I would talk to you the way we do on the phone and say the hotter-than fuck things that make you moan my name as you come, then turn around and go out with someone else?"

She swallowed hard. "I don't know what I think," she answered honestly, hating that vulnerable note of emotion in her voice. The doubts and insecurities. "I just know that the men in my past haven't always taken my feelings into consideration when it comes to relationships. Not that I'm calling what we do a relationship, it's just that . . . " Her voice trailed off, because she was at a loss over what to say next.

His jaw clenched with frustration. "Just for the record, I'm not like Brice, or any of the other idiots who came before him who didn't know a good thing when they had it. And I don't screw around with other women when I'm focused on the one I want. And to ease your mind, Julia doesn't do a thing for me, because all I can think about is wanting *you*. I've had *one* relationship since our night in Denver over three and a half years ago and it was very short-lived, and you want to know why?" he asked as his fingers slid around the side of her neck and he drew her face, her mouth even closer to his. "Because I've compared every woman to you, and they *always* come up lacking. So do *not* doubt what you feel between us is real. You just need to let that guard of yours down and give what's still between us a chance. Can you *try* and do that?"

He wasn't asking her for a commitment, which she wasn't sure she was capable of giving him when she'd never personally had a relationship with staying power, anyway. And truthfully, resisting Connor was getting more and more difficult, and taking that next logical step to just give in to what they both wanted and desired— each other—was easier than fighting their attraction when they were near one another.

She just had to be careful to keep her heart

and emotions out of the equation, and just enjoy her baby daddy with benefits. "Yes, I can try."

Chapter Eight

CONNOR FINISHED WASHING the last of the dishes in Katie's sink, trying to help out where he could while she gave Val a bath and got her ready for bed. For the most part, everything was put away and cleaned up, thanks to Avery staying to help speed up the process.

But now everyone was gone for the evening, and after four hours of continuous birthday festivities and activities, Val had been smudged with dirt, sticky from cake and candy, as well a little grumpy from being so exhausted. Connor had witnessed his first toddler tantrum and meltdown when Katie had to take away the soft, plush unicorn that he'd given to Val as one of her gifts since it couldn't go in the tub with her.

The corner of his mouth twitched with a

grin as he recalled the way his daughter had flung her little body onto the living room floor and kicked her feet while bawling crocodile tears and crying, "I want it, I want it," while Katie tried to reason with her. It had taken major effort for Connor to school his expression so he didn't die laughing at the little girl's dramatic display. Seeing it all for the first time, he thought it was funny and adorable, though Katie had failed to see the humor in it— probably because she was as tired as Val.

But things had quieted down in the bathroom once Katie had gotten Val in the tub. He heard them talking quietly, and though he couldn't hear what they were saying, he was in complete awe of Katie's toddler-whispering skills that had calmed their daughter and had her cooperating again.

As he finished wiping down the counter, Katie came into the kitchen looking a little fatigued, and he walked right up to her and pulled her into a hug, just because she looked like she could use one. There was the barest hint of hesitation before she gave herself over to the affectionate embrace and slid her arms around his waist, leaning into him. It was a small, trusting gesture, but he'd take it.

He rubbed his hands up and down her back and smiled against the head she'd rested on his chest. "Someone's a little cranky tonight."

She glanced up at him, a delicate brow raised incredulously. "You'd better not be talking about me," she said, though there was a playfulness in her tone.

He chuckled. "I wasn't, but even if I were, I know exactly how to make your grumpies go away." He gave her a sexy, meaningful wink that made her cheeks go pink, then loosened his hold. "Now it's your turn to go and take a nice, hot shower. I'll go say good night to Val and make sure there's nothing left outside or on the patio that needs to be put away."

"Connor, you don't have to do that," she said with a shake of her head. "Whatever's not done, I'll finish up tomorrow sometime."

"I want to do it." She was so used to doing everything herself, and he wanted to lighten her burden where he could. "Remember that conversation we had about having someone taking care of you for a change? Let me do that for you tonight, okay?" He'd let her interpret that any way she wanted, because if the opportunity presented itself, he definitely wanted to take care of her in more ways than one.

She smiled at him, her expression grateful. "Okay. Thank you."

"You're welcome." He placed a soft, chaste kiss on her forehead. "Now go."

He followed Katie down the short hallway, and when she disappeared into her bedroom, he slipped into Val's. The overhead light was off, though the room was illuminated by the glow of a nightlight on the small table beside her bed. She was already passed out, and even though Connor would have liked for her to see him one more time before she'd fallen asleep, he knew the fun-filled day had completely worn her out.

Pushing his hands into the pockets of his jeans, he stood there for a few minutes taking in the long lashes that framed her closed eyelids, the pink parted lips drawing in even breaths, and her sweet, serene expression as she slept. He'd only known about Val for a short time, but he already knew that this little girl held his heart, and that he loved her unconditionally, with a fierce protectiveness he never knew was possible. He would, undoubtedly, slay dragons for her . . . and kick any guy's ass in the future who dared to make her cry.

She had a choke hold on the plush unicorn he'd bought for her under one of her arms. The moment she'd pulled it out of the gift bag and seen the gold horn on its forehead and the rainbow-colored mane and tail that shimmered in the sunlight, her eyes had sparkled with such delight. She'd hugged and kissed the soft stuffed animal, had immediately named her Sparkles, and wouldn't part with it for the rest of the party. Well, until her little conniption fit right before her bath.

He grinned to himself. He didn't know if she was so attached to the unicorn because it resembled one of her My Little Ponies or if it was because he'd given it to her, but it didn't really matter. He was definitely winning over his little girl. Now, it was time to work on her mother.

He bent down and ran his fingertips along her downy-soft cheek, and she didn't so much as stir. "Good night, sweet girl," he murmured, then left her room, closing the door quietly behind him.

He walked through the backyard, picking up a few things here and there, then came back inside and made sure everything was locked up. He turned off the lights and made his way to Katie's bedroom. Once inside, he closed her door and after making sure the monitor on the night table was on for Val, he turned the lock. The shower was off, and he heard Katie moving around in the bathroom, so he sat down at the foot of her bed to wait for her to come out.

What happened next with Katie, if anything at all, was completely up to her. If she wanted him to leave, he would. If she asked him to cuddle with her on the bed because she was exhausted, well, holding her close for a few hours certainly wouldn't be a hardship. And if she was ready to make all those orgasms he'd given her over the phone a reality, he was totally on board with making her relax in the best way possible, too.

Bottom line, he'd respect any decision she made.

A few minutes later, the bathroom door opened and she walked out, dressed in a tank top and pajama short set that was faded and well-worn. The very ends of her blonde hair that brushed along her shoulders were damp from her shower, and her face was scrubbed clean of any makeup, though her skin looked soft and luminescent, and as she neared, she brought with her the fragrance of her body wash—delicious apples and warm honey.

She stopped a few feet away and gave him a

self-conscious but wry smile. "So . . . this is me in all my mom glory." She indicated her comfortable, practical nightwear. "It's not always pretty, well put together, or glamorous."

He let his gaze travel down the length of her, taking in the full, bare breasts beneath the cotton material and the gorgeous, toned legs that extended from the end of her shorts before raising his eyes back up to her face. His cock was already thickening behind the fly of his jeans, wanting her just the way she was. He didn't need sexy lingerie on her body to make him hard. His desire for her was based on how good he already knew it felt to be buried deep inside her. Three and a half years later, and he still remembered . . . and apparently, so did his dick.

"Trust me, I like you like this just fine. *More* than fine, actually." He pushed to his feet and closed the distance between them, until he was standing right in front of her and she had to tip her head back slightly to meet his gaze. "You totally fucking rock the mom look."

She laughed softly. "You're such a sweet-talker."

He pushed his hands into her hair and brought her head toward him, until her hands were pressed against his chest and his mouth was right up against her ear. "You know I'm not always a sweet-talker," he said huskily. "In fact, you prefer when I talk dirty, don't you?"

"I like you both ways," she told him, her warm breath caressing his cheek. "Sweet *and* dirty."

He chuckled and tightened his fingers in her hair to tip her head back again, the awareness flickering in her gaze giving him hope. "Sweet is reserved for outside of the bedroom, because what I want to do to you in the privacy of this room is in no way, shape, or form *sweet*. It's dirty and filthy and so indecent you'll want to spread your legs wider, claw at the bed sheets, and beg me for more."

She shivered, her lashes falling half-mast and her lips parting in invitation. "Connor . . . "

It wasn't the unconditional *yes* he was looking for to move forward, but it wasn't an obvious *no*, either.

"Open your eyes and look at me, Katie," he said, and waited until her dark brown eyes focused on his before he continued. "If you tell me you don't want this, if you tell me to go, I will and we'll wait until you're ready. But make your decision fast, otherwise I'm going to strip you naked and touch you and kiss you and make you come with my mouth so hard you'll see stars . . . and then I'm going to fuck you like I've been dying to do since the moment I saw you again at the restaurant." He skimmed his thumb along the lush bottom lip he wanted to taste, the mouth he'd fantasized about fucking. "Stay or go? What's it going to be, Katie?"

The tip of her tongue slowly, boldly touched the pad of his finger, and Jesus Christ, he felt that lick all the way down to his stiff, aching cock.

"I want this . . . " she whispered, the look in her eyes both vulnerable and daring at the same time. "I want *you*."

He groaned in profound relief, not because this was about finally having sex with her. No, it was all about taking that next step toward building intimacy with this woman he cared so much about already, and gaining her trust. More than anything, he wanted that.

He brought her mouth to his in a soft, indulgent, getting-to-know-you-again kiss that elicited a sigh of longing from her that resonated in him, as well. Eventually, he increased the pressure of his lips against hers, and like a sweet, blossoming flower, she opened to him and greeted the seductive sweep of his tongue with her own.

She made an arousing sound in the back of her throat, her fingers fisting in his T-shirt and her hips shifting restlessly against his as he devoured her mouth slowly, deeply, passionately. He tipped her head one way, then another, their damp lips sliding erotically, their tongues tangling carnally. They kissed like that for long, endless minutes, letting their desire build and enjoying that first time all over again.

When he finally lifted his mouth from hers, her lashes fluttered open to look up at him, and the laid-bare smile that eased across her lips stirred something inside his chest. Made his desire for her stronger, made what they were about to do more intimate.

"I missed you," he said, the words traveling from his brain to his mouth before he could stop them. But it was true. They might have only spent one night together in Denver, but she'd put an indelible mark on his heart that was clearly still there.

"I missed you, too," she admitted, touching her fingers to the stubble on his jaw, for the moment her defenses down. "I didn't think it was possible, only knowing you for such a short time, but I thought about you every day."

He let go of her face and settled his hands on her hips. "And at night?"

Her cheeks blushed a pretty shade of pink. "Yeah, I thought about you then, too, and remembered all the ways . . . "

"I fucked you?" he supplied for her, a rogue grin on his lips as he slid his hands beneath the hem of her tank top. She shivered when his fingers touched her bare skin, her nipples pebbling against where they were pressed to his chest.

"Yeah," she admitted, her breath catching as he continued skimming his palms up toward her breasts. "You were pretty thorough."

She shuddered when he placed warm, suctioning kisses along the side of her neck. "And Jesus, Katie, you were so willing and eager and so damn easy to please." He blew a stream of hot breath along her damp skin. "You were so responsive and needy, like you couldn't get enough."

"That was all your fault," she said, and moaned when he finally filled his hands with her luscious breasts.

"My fault?" he murmured, though he was more than happy to take the blame for something that had benefited both of them at the time. "How do you figure?"

"I've never been that way with anyone else," she said huskily, her confession making his dick swell thicker, harder. "No one has ever made me feel as hot and sexy as you did, so it was easy to just let go and enjoy everything you did to me."

Yeah, every guy before him had been a fucking fool. Then again, if it hadn't been for the last idiot she'd been in Denver to surprise, he never would have met Katie. And that was something he didn't even want to think about.

"Baby, your body was *made* for a man to pleasure. Let me show you . . . that is, if you don't mind me testing that theory out on you," he teased.

She laughed lightly. "Umm, I think I'm okay with that."

Withdrawing his hands from beneath her top, he led her to the foot of the bed. He sat down on the edge of the mattress and drew her toward him, until she was standing between his spread legs.

"Take off your top for me," he said, wanting to enjoy the sexy striptease right in front of him.

Her fingers toyed with the hem but didn't lift it yet. "Only if you do, too."

He chuckled. "Fair enough."

He divested himself of his shirt in record time, not wanting to miss a second of her peeling that fabric up along her torso, revealing her smooth stomach and the most gorgeous breasts he'd ever laid his eyes on—well, since Denver, anyway. They seemed bigger than he remembered, her curves more pronounced, probably because of having a baby, and those changes in her body only added to her allure.

Heat and lust pumped through him, and he had to inhale a deep breath to keep himself under a modicum of control. "Come a little closer," he said. "So those perfect breasts are right at my mouth level."

Placing her hands on his shoulders, she inched forward, closing any gaps between them, and shamelessly brushed a pebbled nipple across his lips, playfully teasing him. His tongue came out and flicked across that beaded tip as he grabbed on to her waist, then gradually slid his palms down and into the waistband of her shorts and panties. She did the same with her other nipple, keeping them just out of mouth's reach, the flirtatious light in her eyes only making him hotter, more determined to win at this little game she was amusing herself with.

While she continued to delight in taunting him—and he was able to get in an occasional lick—he tugged the rest of her clothes over her hips and shoved them down her legs, baring the rest of her body.

She gasped in surprise, clearly not paying attention to what *he'd* been doing. "Oh, you're good."

He grinned up at her while trailing his fingers up along the backs of her thighs, until he reached her ass, which he squeezed in his hands. "I've got way more smooth moves than you do, sweetheart."

"Yeah?" She arched a dubious brow, still so seductively mischievous. "Show me what you've got, Mr. Prescott."

"Gladly." Splaying one of his palms in the middle of her back gave him the control he needed to force her to arch her chest forward, and as soon as her breasts were literally in his face, he latched on to a nipple and sucked hard and deep. Startled by the rough scrape of his teeth, she tangled her hands in his hair and tried to pull him back, but he didn't budge, nor did he relent with his swirling licks and hot, wet, nibbling bites that would definitely leave marks of possession on her pale skin.

She swallowed back a desperate whimper, her fingers twisting the strands of his hair so tight his scalp burned. "Oh, God, Connor . . . "

He pushed his free hand between her legs and groaned around her breast as the slick heat of her pussy greeted him. Thrusting two fingers deep inside of her core, he began fucking her just like that, while his thumb rubbed her clit, providing the pressure and friction she needed to make that climb toward her first release.

She started to pant and writhe against him, but the hand still on her back kept her right where he wanted her, unable to escape until he was ready to let her. Her hips rocked uninhibitedly against his hand, matching the rhythm of his pumping fingers as she chased the orgasm he knew she was on the verge of grasping. He pushed deeper, finding the spot that would definitely propel her over the edge, and he stroked it, again and again, intensifying the sensation until she was moaning and her body started to tremble and shake.

She cried out, much louder than he'd anticipated, and he prayed to God that Val was a sound sleeper, and was relieved when he heard nothing from the monitor in the room. Katie's sex clenched tight around his fingers, her pleasure so intense she went up on her tiptoes to escape the relentless action of his thumb against that sensitive nub of flesh, to release the hard, biting suction of his mouth on her nipple, but he followed, forcing her to ride out the climax pulsing through her and prolonging the exquisite torture until he knew he'd wrung every last ounce of ecstasy from her.

As soon as he released her breast and withdrew his fingers, she leaned into him, her legs buckling. He caught her around the waist and moved so he could put her down on the bed. She scooted up toward the pillows and waited for him to join her. He opened the front of his jeans, but before he pushed them off, he realized there was a conversation they needed to have before they went any further.

He met her gaze, trying to keep his eyes off her gorgeous, naked body. "I have a condom in my wallet, and considering what happened in Denver . . . are you back on some kind of birth control?"

She nodded. "I'm on the pill, mostly to regulate my periods. And I haven't been with anyone since you."

"It's been almost a year for me, and I'm clean," he told her, just so she knew, and pulled his wallet from his jeans to retrieve the condom.

Quickly stripping off the rest of his clothes, he rolled on the protection and climbed up onto the bed, stopping when he was kneeling in the inviting spread of Katie's legs. His cock jutted straight up, hard as a spike, and it didn't help matters that she was staring at his dick like she wanted to swallow it whole. He groaned inwardly. Bad analogy, because yeah, they were going to get around to that eventually.

Her gaze moved up his body appreciatively while he did the same to hers, but in the opposite direction. His perusal stopped when he saw a thin line of a scar low on her abdomen that hadn't been there in Denver, and his instincts told him that it had something to do with her pregnancy.

It was the only thing that made sense, but if he was wrong, he wanted to know. "What is this scar from?" he asked, touching it gently with a finger.

She exhaled a breath. "They had to take Val in an emergency c-section."

A rush of emotions hit him hard, along with a whole lot of regrets, and he exhaled through the tightening in his gut. He still didn't know the details of Val's birth, but now wasn't the time to have the conversation. But they would at some point.

"If you're waiting for an invitation to continue testing your theory about pleasuring me, you have one," Katie said, opting for a lighthearted comment to get things back to where they were, which he appreciated.

Putting his thoughts back on her, he grinned wickedly and picked up one of her legs. Holding her curious gaze, he placed a sizzling, open-mouthed kiss on the inside of her knee, then continued with a whole lot more of them up her inner thigh—kissing, licking, gently biting his way toward her hot, wet center—still swollen and sensitive from her first orgasm of the night.

She squirmed against the comforter, and when he was good and settled between her legs and was one wet kiss away from her pussy, she reached down and pressed her hands along the tops of his shoulders to keep him from reaching his destination.

"Connor, no," she begged, her fingers digging into his muscles. "I can't. Not again."

With his arms keeping her thighs spread open for him, he grasped her wrists and pulled her hands away, pinning them against her sides so she had no choice but to give herself over to him. "Oh, yeah, you can," he countered, running his tongue along her slit and reveling in her full-body tremble. "You *will*," he added, knowing he could take her up a second time, because he'd done so that night in Denver, multiple times.

He circled her clit, soft and slow, the wild whimper that escaped her throat telling him that while her mouth might protest, her pussy was totally on board with another orgasm. "I want you right back on the edge, baby, so when I fuck you, I'll feel you come around my cock."

Done talking, he gave all his attention to the task at hand, and before long her hips were arching up to meet the swirl of his tongue and she was begging for that second release she'd sworn she didn't have in her to give.

With her at the peak once again, and his cock throbbing for the feel of her body, hot and tight, gripping him, he released her hands and reared up and over her, burying himself balls deep in one hard, driving thrust that wrenched a gasp of shock from Katie. That moment of adjustment quickly unraveled into a needy moan as her inner walls began pulsing around him.

He saw the raw, unbridled passion in her eyes, and a reciprocating lust and desire spread through him like wildfire. The feel of her wrapped so tight around his shaft was all too much and yet not enough. She clutched his shoulders and arched beneath him, and Jesus fuck, he slid impossibly deeper, groaning as her slick heat coated every inch of his dick as she came undone.

He was right behind her. Hitching her legs high around his waist for an even better angle, he buried his hands in her hair, pulling her head back as he crushed his mouth over hers, his tongue demanding, claiming, and possessing. The same way he branded her body, completely and utterly, his climax roaring through him as he rode her so fucking hard and deep he was surprised he didn't split her in two.

When they were both spent, he moved off of her and went to the bathroom to clean up. When he returned, he pulled her close to his side, refusing to let her retreat from him, emotionally or physically. Luckily, she cuddled into him, resting her head on his chest, with one of her legs entwined around his and a hand resting on his stomach.

He pulled the sheet up to their waists and

gave her a few moments to relax, to let the adrenaline rush of her second orgasm subside before he brought up the scar again. He didn't want to leave until he knew everything that had happened to her and Val.

Very gently, he threaded his fingers through her silky hair, enjoying the feel of her warm body pressed so intimately to his. "Katie, what caused Val to be born prematurely?"

He felt her inhale a deep breath against his ribs, then release it slowly. "In my seventh month, there was a complication in my pregnancy. It's called placental abruption, and it's where the placental lining separates from the uterus, which can ultimately deprive the baby of oxygen and nutrients. It's not completely uncommon, and if it's caught early it can be monitored closely with bed rest, but unfortunately, by the time I had any noticeable symptoms, it was nearly a total separation and they had to take her by emergency c-section."

"How did you know?" he asked curiously.

She absently rubbed her hand up and down his stomach, while he kneaded her scalp with his fingers. "Well . . . I was just into my seventh month, and it started with occasional abdominal pain and my back started to ache. I honestly thought it was indigestion, and since I had an appointment the next day with my doctor, I figured I'd talk to him about the issue when I saw him. Except I woke up in the middle of the night with continuous contractions and I was bleeding. A lot."

He could only imagine how scared she'd been, all alone by herself. "I take it you called an ambulance?"

"No, I called Avery," she said with a light laugh. "Leah was less than a year old at that time, and in my panic, I figured she'd know what was going on. I remember her saying, *That's not good*, and she came right over and immediately took me to the hospital, while her husband stayed home with the baby."

"I'm glad she was there for you," he said quietly, knowing that she had no family she could rely on, though he truly hated that he hadn't been able to take care of her.

"Me, too. Avery kept me calm, and as soon as a doctor came in to examine me, I was taken immediately into the OR for a c-section. Less than fifteen minutes later, Val was born, at three pounds, six ounces."

"Wow," he breathed, thinking of how *tiny* that was. She probably would have fit into the palm of his hand.

"The hard part was that I couldn't hold her right away," Katie went on. "She was taken directly to NICU, and the next time I saw her she was in an incubator and hooked up to a bunch of tubes. She looked so little and frail, and I was so scared that she wasn't going to make it."

He heard the helpless emotion in Katie's voice, and he hugged her closer, and she let him. "Clearly, our little girl is a fighter."

Katie nodded against his chest. "That she is. She was able to come home after almost a month in NICU."

He couldn't stop the regrets that eased through him. "I wish I could have been there for you and Val. It's hard, realizing I missed out on three years of her life." It was something he'd never be able to get back.

"I know," she said in understanding, the empathy in her voice genuine. "I'm sorry you missed all that time with her, too."

He didn't like asking the next question, but if there were any lingering issues, he wanted to know. "With her being born early, have there been any . . . developmental concerns?"

She lifted her head and propped her chin on

the hand she'd slid up to his chest. "For the first year, she was a little behind on her milestones, but nothing that overly concerned her pediatrician. By her second year, she was nearly caught up, and now, she's a little *ahead* of where she should be, mentally and physically."

"Ahhh, that's my girl," he said, unable to keep the pride from his voice.

Katie pursed her lips at him, though her eyes sparkled humorously. "I suppose next you're going to tell me that with all that brains and beauty, she takes after the Prescott side."

"No," he said, though he was still smiling. "So far, I think she's a great combination of both of us."

"And that tantrum she had earlier?" She raised a brow. "Where does that stubbornness come from?"

He smirked, because clearly she believed it came from *him*. "You say that like stubbornness is a bad thing."

"It is when it's coming from a three-year-old in the form of a temperamental fit."

He moved to his side so their heads were each on a pillow and they were now face-to-face. "Hey, I'd be cranky, too, if I was exhausted and coming down from a major sugar high and someone took away my favorite toy."

She laughed and pinched him playfully on his stomach, which made his dick twitch at that bit of pleasurable pain. "Oh, my God. Already, you're a soft touch."

"With Val? Yeah, it's hard not to be," he admitted, because his daughter totally fascinated and charmed him. Grabbing Katie's hand, he flattened her palm and guided it downward, watching as her eyes gradually darkened when she realized what he was doing. "Now her mother, on the other hand, makes me very, very hard." He wrapped her fingers around his stiff cock, and with his hand over hers, he helped her stroke his shaft slowly, rhythmically.

Seductively holding his gaze, she squeezed his erection and skimmed her thumb over the head while licking her tongue along her bottom lip that had a very naughty, tempting curve to it.

He groaned as his imagination went wild, as she no doubt intended. He slid his free hand along the side of her neck and used his thumb to push past her lips, her teeth, and felt his cock throb when she sucked on his finger. "Jesus, that mouth of yours, Katie," he said in a gravelly, aroused voice. "You already know that I want to do bad, dirty things to it. This isn't helping matters any."

"Maybe I *want* you to do bad, dirty things to my mouth," she said, letting go of his erection so she could push him to his back and make good on her promise.

Starting at his chest, she kissed and licked her way down his body as she knelt between his legs, which he'd eagerly spread for her. The tips of her hair trailed along his stomach, his thighs, and *dear fucking God*, the hot, exquisite feel of her mouth enveloping him, inch by aching inch, had his goddamn toes curling and the muscles in his abs tightening.

He was long and thick, and it was sheer, blissful torture as she used her lips and tongue all along his shaft, making him leak pre-come and teasing him to the point that he fisted his hand in her hair so that he was now in control. Her mouth came over him again, her soft lips stroking down his shaft, and he thrust in counterpoint, meeting the back of her throat.

She moaned eagerly around his cock, which he felt all the way up his spine. She swallowed him deep and sucked him hard as he guided her head back up, then down . . . again and again, until the rapidly increasing tension in his groin demanded release and holding back any longer wasn't an option.

Out of courtesy, he tried to lift her greedy mouth away, but she wouldn't let him. She went down on him again, *all the fucking way*, those soft lips tightening around him as he instinctively pumped his hips forward and came against the back of her throat with a harsh, guttural, shuddering groan that reverberated throughout his entire body. That fantasy he'd shared with her on the phone, she totally made it a reality, and it was far hotter than his filthy mind had even imagined.

When he finally gained his bearings, she was up by him again, a satisfied grin on her face, the little vixen. "Give me a second, and I'll totally repay the favor."

She shook her head as she placed a kiss on his jaw. "That's not why I did it. I *wanted* to. Besides, I already had my two orgasms, so I'm all good."

Smiling back at her, he pushed his fingers into her hair and gently brought her head down to lie on his chest. Beyond relaxed, he closed his eyes again and enjoyed the perfect intimacy of being with Katie like this.

"Connor . . . " she said softly when minutes had passed, her head lifting from his chest.

"You know you can't stay, right?"

Hearing the uncertainty in her voice, he opened his eyes and stared into hers, realizing that while he'd been able to break down one wall with Katie tonight—the physical connection—there were still many more for him to hurdle to gain her complete trust.

"I wasn't going to stay," he told her, because he knew she wasn't ready for sleepovers or having to explain to her daughter why Connor had stayed the night. And honestly, he respected that, and Katie, enough to abide by those rules for now.

Chapter Nine

K ATIE KEPT AN eye on the digital clock on her computer as she worked on a full-page ad for a local business that was due to the client in two days while trying to block out the sound of her lawn guy mowing the grass in the front and back yards. Val would be home soon from her playdate with Leah for the afternoon, which had given Katie some much-needed quiet time to concentrate on the commissioned piece without interruptions, and Connor was due to arrive, too, with pizza for dinner.

Tonight was a big night for all of them, and Katie would be lying if she said she wasn't nervous about finally telling Val that Connor was her daddy. Knowing that every moment he'd spent with the little girl had been leading up to this moment didn't make it any easier for Katie to face, but she'd made peace with the fact that she'd be sharing Val with a man who clearly adored the ground the little girl walked on, and eventually, she'd meet his family, too.

Since Val's birthday party a week and a half ago, Connor had made every effort to spend as much time with Val as he could to build his relationship with her and establish a routine Val looked forward to. Mostly, that was on the weekends or in the early evenings, after he got off work and before their daughter's bedtime. He'd either take them out to dinner or Katie would cook for them, and afterward he'd sit on the floor and play with whatever toys Val brought out from her room. There were even a few nights that they'd all gone over to his place to eat, so his daughter was comfortable at his house, too.

They watched Disney movies together with Val usually curled up to his side, and Connor now knew all the lyrics to "Let it Go" and sang it out loud with Val when it came on, which always made Katie laugh because they were both so off-key. When Val was finally tucked in bed for the night with Sparkles the unicorn, he'd read her a story from one of her favorite books, then kiss her good night.

And then, when Val was asleep, he'd kiss Katie *hello*, which usually ended up with them in a hot make-out session or in the bedroom with Connor deep inside of her, making her feel things—intimate, emotional things—that she was struggling to keep compartmentalized so she didn't end up getting hurt down the line. She was trying to be smart and sensible when it came to their arrangement.

The situation felt so perfect, like that "honeymoon phase" of a relationship, when everything was wonderful and shiny and happy. But in her experience, that never lasted, and there was no denying the one common denominator in all those previously failed relationships was *her*. The one thing that kept her from letting her guard down completely with Connor was knowing that any issues between the two of them would directly affect Val, and Katie would do anything to protect her little girl from the kind of unstable and painful childhood she'd had. It was safer to keep things as simple and as casual as possible between them.

Mentally, she knew it was the most practical thing to do, but her heart was definitely having a hard time trying to stick to that particular game plan.

The doorbell rang, pulling her from her wandering thoughts, and she cringed when she realized she'd wasted twenty minutes in her own head, rather than on the ad she needed to finish. Knowing she'd have to get more work done tonight after Val was asleep and Connor was gone, she shut down her computer and made her way to the front door. She smoothed a hand down the front of the pretty dress she'd worn, all too aware of that giddy sensation in the pit of her stomach at the thought of seeing Connor.

She opened her door with a huge smile on her face, which quickly faded when she found Garrett, her lawn guy, standing there instead, his mower and leaf blower on the sidewalk leading up to the house. The yard looked immaculate, like always when he was done, and she'd already paid him for the month, so maybe there was a problem of some sort he had to tell her about?

"Hey, Garrett," she said, coming out onto the porch. "Is everything okay?"

"With your lawn? Yeah, everything is fine," he assured her with a smile that was friendly but more direct than usual, as was the way he moved a bit closer. "Actually, I was hoping we could talk for a few minutes, non-business-related?"

Oh, crap. She'd forgotten all about Avery telling Garrett that she was single and available. The last few times he'd come to do the yard, she hadn't been home, so he clearly was taking the opportunity to approach her now. A sense of dread trickled through her, because the last thing she wanted was to have this conversation with him, which would undoubtedly lead to having to reject any overture he made. Yet she couldn't very well say, *No, I don't want to talk,* either.

"Sure," she said instead, keeping her voice casual even as she saw Connor pull up to the curb and get out of his truck with two boxes of pizza balanced in one of his hands. "What's up?"

"I was talking to your neighbor a few weeks ago, and she mentioned you were single and not seeing anyone," he said, his eyes filled with undeniable interest. "And I thought maybe you and I could go out on a date sometime?"

Behind him, Connor was making his way up the walkway, his stride definitely more purposeful than usual, though the man in front of Katie wasn't paying attention to anything but her. "Garrett, that's really nice of you to ask, but I'm going to have to say no."

"Ahh, come on, Katie." His voice was persuasive as he unexpectedly reached out and grabbed her hand, holding it tight in his as he rubbed his thumb across her knuckles. "Give a guy a chance. I guarantee you'll have a good time." He winked at her.

Ugh. She was already giving one guy a chance, but even if she wasn't, Garrett just didn't do anything for her. God, no other man would ever *do it* for her like Connor did, and she'd known that since that night in Denver.

She was trying to find a nice way to turn him down, but the fact that Connor now had a ferocious frown on his face as he approached was distracting the heck out of her. She tried to retrieve her hand as gracefully as possible, but Garrett clearly wasn't ready to let go.

"Is there a problem here?" Connor asked gruffly as he made his way up the porch stairs, his chest puffed out in a way she'd never seen before, which made his shoulders look broader and his body language more intimidating.

Garrett was initially startled by Connor's sudden appearance and demanding question since he hadn't seen him coming, but he quickly recovered and gave Connor an equally aggressive glare. "No, there's no problem here."

Connor, usually so easygoing, looked pointedly at where Garrett still had a hold on her, his gaze laser hot. "If there isn't a problem, then I suggest you let go of her hand before I do it for you."

Jesus, the testosterone in the air was so thick she could have cut it with a knife. The two men were sizing each other up, never having met each other, and Katie opened her mouth to tell Connor that she was *fine* so he'd cool his jets, but Garrett spoke first.

"You're the fucking pizza delivery guy," he mocked incredulously, clearly misconstruing the boxes in Connor's hand. "What the hell business is it of yours *what* I do with this woman?"

Connor went from merely uptight to livid. "Because I'm not the fucking pizza delivery guy, you asshole," he said, stepping closer to Garrett. "I'm Val's *father*, and if you touch Katie again, I'll break your fucking arm."

Garrett's hold on her finally loosened, and she pulled her hand back and immediately pressed it to Connor's chest, trying to keep him from moving forward any more and to hopefully calm him. "*Connor*, everything is fine. He's the guy who does my lawn."

"Not anymore," Connor said without missing a beat. "Thank you for your services, but I'll be mowing her grass and taking care of her yard from now on."

Then he promptly grabbed Katie's elbow and steered her back into the house, kicking the door shut after them. He released her arm and Katie stared at him in disbelief as he walked into the kitchen and set the pizza boxes on the counter. She crossed her arms over her chest, and when he turned back around and saw her giving him a *what the hell* kind of look, his posture turned defensive.

"What?" he asked in a gravelly voice, like he'd done nothing out of the ordinary, or wrong.

She shook her head as she moved into the kitchen, letting her annoyance surface. "Don't you think you went a little overboard out there? He is, *was*, my landscaper!"

He braced his hands on his hips, and she was both in awe and annoyed with this alpha side to Connor. "I'm more than capable of taking care of your yard for you."

"What if I don't want you to?" she said, her

own temper rising, because the last thing she wanted was to rely on him to take care of her. Val depending on him was one thing because he was her father, but it was a luxury Katie refused to get used to. "It's not up to you to decide who I hire to do anything around here. It's my house."

"He was coming on to you," Connor argued, obviously not liking what he'd seen out on the porch. "What kind of professional does that?"

She tried to explain Garrett's reasons for approaching her. "Avery told him I was single and available, and he was just asking me out based on that information."

A muscle in Connor's jaw clenched as he stalked toward her. "Avery did *what*?"

She took a step back as he neared, and found herself backed up against the counter. "She told him that *before* I found you," she clarified so he didn't think Avery was currently soliciting dates for her with Connor in the picture. "Before you and I . . . " God, what did she call this thing between them?

He braced those sturdy, muscled arms on the counter on either side of her, their bodies so close she could feel the heat radiating off his chest, could see the possessive spark in his gaze that made her go weak in the knees, and dear God, made her shamelessly wet.

His gorgeous dark blue eyes bored into hers. "Before you and I *what*, Katie?" he demanded, forcing her to define their relationship.

And still, she couldn't come up with one single word to describe what they were doing, because they weren't dating, they weren't a couple ... hell, they weren't even technically exclusive. So, she stated the obvious. "Before you and I started sleeping together."

He didn't seem all that happy with her answer. In fact, he appeared even more frustrated. "Yeah, well, while we're *sleeping together*, you're mine. I don't fucking share."

He cupped the back of her head in one of his big hands as his mouth crashed down on hers, capturing the startled gasp that escaped from her throat as his firm lips parted hers without any sweet preliminaries and his tongue pushed deep. No, this kiss was hot and hard and possessive from the get-go, the fingers gripping her scalp giving him all the control and giving her no choice but to surrender to his mouth. To him.

She did. Eagerly and willingly, her body inevitably craving his. He yanked up the hem of her dress with his free hand, and she moaned when he slid his hand between her legs. His strong fingers rubbed along her drenched panties and his thumb pressed hard and firm against her clit through the silk fabric, sending jolts of need pulsing through her sex as his mouth ravaged hers and his touch made her think of only one thing: feeling him inside of her, filling her full and easing the ache building between her thighs.

Her hands dropped to the waistband of his jeans, working the top button open, then unzipping the fly. She reached inside his briefs. He was like a thick, steel rod in her hand, and she wrapped him in her fist and stroked him the same way he was sliding his fingers against her pussy. A generous bead of fluid leaked from the tip of his cock, and she slicked it over the head, earning her a deep, ragged groan from him as he thrust his shaft in the tight clasp of her hand.

Desire slammed through her, and she rocked her hips against his fingers, wanting, *needing* to come. But instead of giving her that release, he tore his mouth from hers and spun her around so he was standing behind her now. He made quick work of shoving her dress up to her waist and tugging her panties down so that they fell to the floor around her feet.

Before she could take her next breath, he pushed his cock along the crease of her bottom, found her slick opening, and entered her in one driving thrust that had her crying out from the force of it. He gripped her hips so hard she was sure he'd leave marks behind, his body pistoning into hers in a fast, hard fuck that had her head spinning and her heart racing.

"*Connor*," she moaned, standing on the tips of her toes and trying to grind back against him for more.

He continued to pound into her. "Put your hands on the counter and push your ass back against me," he demanded, his voice a low rasp of sound that was rich with lust and sent chills of excitement through her. "I want as deep as I can get."

She obeyed his order, bending her upper body and using the counter as leverage as she tipped her bottom higher for him, gasping as the angle seemed to gain him another inch inside her. He came over her from behind, aligning their bodies, from their thighs to his chest pressing against her back. One of his hands slid down her stomach and returned between her legs, catching her aching clit between two fingers and tugging rhythmically, while his other hand slid around her throat, tipping her head back so his mouth was against her cheek, his ragged breaths hot and damp against her skin.

He held her firm and immobile, taking her with a passion so fierce it branded her soul, while fucking her like he had a point to prove, that she was his. She couldn't move even if she tried . . . and Lord help her, she didn't want to. She'd never felt so possessed, so completely and utterly dominated, and as soon as her orgasm crashed through her, she felt Connor lose control behind her, his thrusts coming shorter, tighter, infinitely deeper as raw, primal grunts filled her ear—hell, the entire kitchen—as he came, too.

They were both panting when it was over, and suddenly Connor went from fairly relaxed to tense behind her. "*Fuck.* I didn't use a condom."

She had an initial surge of panic. They'd been so wild and frantic for one another that it hadn't crossed her mind, either. But she assured herself that she was on the pill and, dear God, what were the chances of her birth control failing her twice?

"It's okay," she said, deciding that she wasn't going to worry and obsess over something that hadn't even happened yet.

He was still inside of her, and he wrapped his arms tight around her waist. "I don't ever want you to not feel safe with me."

She swallowed hard, because Connor was the first person she'd ever felt safe *with*. "I know. I'm on the pill. Everything should be fine."

"Knock knock," came Avery's deliberately loud voice from the front room. "Anyone home? I've got a special delivery for you."

Oh, shit, Val was home! A second round of panic sent a jolt of adrenaline though Katie's veins, and she and Connor quickly jumped apart just as Katie heard Val say to Avery, "you don't need to hold my hand. We're in my house."

Jesus, Avery probably knew something was going on and was stalling Val's entrance. Katie yanked her panties back up and pushed her dress down while Connor fastened his jeans in record speed, then stepped over to the sink to wash his hands.

"Hey, we're in the kitchen," Katie called out, her voice still a little husky, and seconds later, Val ran into the room . . . and bypassed her mother to run to Connor, who turned just in time from drying his hands to catch her in his arms.

"Hey, princess," he said affectionately, his new pet name for her, which the little girl loved.

Val placed her little hands on his cheeks, a big smile on her face. "Connor! I missed you!" she said, as if she didn't see him every single day. "Push me on my swing?" she asked of the swing set he'd bought for her as part of her birthday present.

He tweaked her cute button nose before putting her back down. "Just a couple of times, then we need to eat dinner. We're having pizza."

"Best day ever!" Val ran out of the kitchen and to the backyard.

Connor gave both women an impish look, clearly aware of what a close call to getting caught that had been. "I'll give you two a few minutes to talk," he said knowingly.

He followed his daughter outside, and Katie glanced at Avery, already feeling her face getting warm. "How long were you out in the living room?"

"Oh, a good minute," her friend said humorously. "I knocked, but when no one answered, I came in, because I saw Connor's truck outside and figured you were home. But then I heard *you know what*, and I had to grab Val's hand before she got an impromptu lesson on the birds and the bees."

Katie winced. "Thank you."

Avery's grin never wavered. "Sounded kind of hot and heavy, and I know all about kid interruptions, so I was just giving you two the courtesy of finishing."

"Would you stop?" Katie shook his head. "Connor came over right when Garrett was asking me out, and that didn't go over well."

"I'd certainly hope not," she replied, laughing. "Did he go all caveman on you?"

Katie blushed more furiously, giving her friend the answer she sought. Desperate to change the subject, she glanced out the kitchen window to the wooden swing set that was now a presence in her backyard. "We're telling Val tonight that Connor is her dad."

Avery came up beside her to look out the window, too. "I don't think that's going to be a problem. Val clearly adores him as much as he adores her."

"I know. It's just . . . I can't help but worry

that it's going to change things. I don't want to lose Val." Even as she said the words, Katie knew that Connor would never take their little girl away from her. But for so long it had just been her and Val, and now that dynamic was shifting and changing to include a third person, so where would that leave *her*?

"You know what I think?" Avery looped her arm through Katie's and didn't wait for a reply. "I think you need to open your eyes a little wider and realize that Connor is the best thing that's ever happened to you, that he's not like all the other guys who came before him."

Katie knew that Connor was different, but a lifetime of insecurities was a harder hurdle to overcome. She knew he'd always be there for Val, but what happened when the novelty of *her* wore off? Because inevitably, that was how all her relationships ended. Why would this one be any different?

KATIE TOOK HER time cleaning up in the kitchen after dinner, knowing what awaited her out in the living room . . . *the talk*. But when she couldn't stall any longer, she headed into the adjoining room, where Connor and Val were playing a game of Hungry Hungry Hippos that she'd received from one of the kids at her birthday party. Even at three years old, it was clear that Val already had a competitive streak, because she was determined to have her hippo eat most of the marbles and her tenacious expression reflected that.

When the play board was cleared and the game over, they each counted out their marbles, and Val came up with three extra over Connor. She jumped up from her kneeling position on the floor, hands raised triumphantly in the air.

"I win, I win!" she shouted happily and laughed at Connor. "That means you lose!"

He grinned at her. "Well, you know what the winner gets?"

Val's eyes grew wide at the thought of getting a prize. "What?"

"Lots and lots of tickles!" Connor lunged for Val, tackling her gently onto the floor where he proceeded to wiggle his fingers against her sides and ribs until the little girl was in a fit of giggles and completely breathless. Only then did he stop.

Katie sat down on the couch as Val rolled to her stomach, propped her chin in her hand, and grinned at Connor. "Let's play again!"

Connor's gaze met Katie's, and they exchanged "the look." "How about in a little bit? Your mom and I want to talk to you first." He got up from the floor and sat next to Katie, then lifted Val so she was sitting on the wooden coffee table in front of both of them.

She sat there, completely guileless, her little legs kicking back and forth. Katie and Connor had agreed that she'd tell Val the news, that it would probably be easier for her to hear, and understand, coming from her mom.

Katie exhaled a deep breath. She'd rehearsed this a dozen times, but that still didn't make this moment any easier. "So, you know how Leah has a mommy and a daddy?"

Val nodded. "I just have a mommy."

Before Katie had seen Connor in the magazine, Val had asked her why she didn't have a daddy, and Katie had replied with "You do have a daddy. He's just not here right now." Which had then prompted Val to respond with, "When will I see him?" And because Katie never wanted Val to feel like she didn't have a daddy, she'd ended the conversation with, "Maybe someday, but for right now, it's just you and me."

Clearly, the day had come.

Katie grabbed her hand, because her own heart was beating so fast and she wanted, *needed* that connection to her daughter in that moment. "Remember when I told you that you did have a daddy, and that someday you'd see him?"

A confused frown marred Val's brows as she nodded again.

A lump of anxiety gathered in Katie's throat, and she had to forcibly swallow it back. "Well . . . Connor is your daddy, sweetheart."

Val's little head immediately jerked to Connor, and she stared at him like she was seeing him for the first time. "*You're* my daddy?"

The emotion in Connor's blue eyes was unmistakable, the love for his little girl distinctly cemented in the bond they already shared. "Yeah, princess, I'm your daddy." His voice was soft but undeniably gruff.

Val jumped down from the table and stepped over to Connor and between his widespread knees. She looked up at him with a heart-melting smile. "I *like* you being my daddy," she said so sweetly it was hard for Katie to breathe. "You're the best daddy ever."

Connor touched his big hand to Val's soft cheek, the moment between father and daughter incredibly tender and precious. "There's something important I want you to know."

"Okay," Val said.

Connor smiled. "I love you, sweet girl."

"I love you, too," Val replied without hesitating, and even though Katie knew her daughter might not realize exactly what those words meant or the depth of emotion they encompassed, she was certain that the little girl would come to love this man as her father, wholly and completely.

Just like Katie was falling in love with Connor. The realization caused both pleasure and pain, because despite her feelings, it didn't change the fact that her trust issues remained.

"On Sunday, I'm taking you and your mommy to dinner, to meet your grandma and grandpa, and your aunt and uncle, too," Connor told her.

"I have a grandma and grandpa?" Val asked in awe, her tiny voice infused with excitement. "I've never had a grandma and grandpa before."

To hear her daughter say that out loud, and knowing that Katie's own parents had shunned this wonderful, beautiful girl who *should have* known a grandparent's love on both sides, made Katie sad. Hopefully Connor's parents would make up for that.

"Well, you do now," Connor said, tapping her playfully on her nose. "And they can't wait to meet you."

Chapter Ten

"**A**RE WE THERE yet?"

Katie glanced to the backseat of the vehicle, where her daughter was buckled into her car seat with Sparkles the unicorn, clearly impatient to get to their destination—Connor's parents' house. They were in Katie's car since there wasn't enough room in his work truck, but Connor had insisted on driving since it would be easier than having her follow his directions, and it also enabled her to converse with Val easily.

"You just asked that question two minutes ago," Katie said with a light laugh.

Val sighed. "I know, but it's so long."

At least one of them was eager to meet Carson and Allison Prescott. Katie was anxious on so many levels that her stomach was in knots. She knew they'd love Val automatically, because she was Connor's child, but how would they feel about *her*? She couldn't seem to stop the insecurities looping through her mind, because she desperately *wanted* his family to like her.

Connor reached across the console and placed his hand on her thigh, giving it a gentle squeeze. "Stop overthinking things, Katie," he murmured so only she could hear. "You look like you're going to throw up."

It amazed her how he could read her so well and so easily. It wasn't the first time he'd been so attuned to her emotions, and she took a deep, calming breath and glanced at him. "It's just nerves. It's been a long time since I've met a guy's parents, and I want to make a good impression, considering I'm the mother of your child."

"You're more than just the mother of my child, Katie," he said with a warm smile, his blue eyes filled with affection. "And my family is equally excited to meet you, too."

You're more than just the mother of my child. He hadn't elaborated on that comment, nor had they officially defined their relationship, though that day out on the front porch with Garrett,

Connor had made it *very* clear that they were exclusive. So, what did that make them? *Exclusive* fuck buddies? She hated the term, because her feelings for Connor had grown beyond mere friendship, and she knew he cared for her, too.

Then again, if he'd insisted on some kind of committed relationship with her, she wasn't sure she was ready to take that next step, or ever would be. Three times burned, and with her parents' history of a nasty divorce with her caught in the middle, and yeah, she was legitimately wary that something this good could last forever. It was easier to protect her heart so when things fizzled, a split wouldn't completely devastate her, especially since Connor would be around for Val for the rest of the little girl's life, whether the two of them were together or not.

"Thank you for bringing Val's baby book," Connor said, interrupting her thoughts. "Everyone is going to love seeing her as a baby, and how much she's grown in the past three years."

"Of course." Connor had already gone through the photos, several times, and Katie knew it would be a great way for his family to feel like they'd at least seen those missing years, along with Val's growth spurts and happy moments, even if they hadn't actually been there.

"Are we there yet *now*?" Val asked again.

Connor glanced in the rearview mirror at his daughter. "Yes, baby girl, we're almost there," he said, his voice amused. "Two more turns, and then I want you to find the house that has the small fountain out front."

"Okay!"

Connor helped Val count the two turns he made onto different streets in the neighborhood he was driving through, and then she searched for the fountain. Connor's parents lived in Wilmette, and he'd told her that they were still in the same house they'd bought when they'd gotten married thirty-two years ago. The same house that Connor and his sister had grown up in.

"There it is, Daddy!" Val exclaimed, pointing toward the well-maintained house with a small gated courtyard out front and a modest, two-tier fountain.

"My mom always wanted a fountain, so my dad bought it for her on their thirtieth anniversary," Connor explained as he pulled up to the curb and parked the car behind a larger SUV, which Katie assumed belonged to his sister and brother-in-law, since they were expected to be here for dinner, as well.

"It's beautiful." And romantic, she thought, awed by how many years his parents had been married.

"Beautiful!" Val repeated, and Katie and Connor laughed.

They got out of the car, with Connor releasing Val from her car seat while Katie gathered her purse and the book of photos she'd brought. Connor and Val led the way with Katie following a few steps behind, since the little girl had automatically latched on to Connor's hand. When they reached the courtyard, Val let go and ran toward the fountain and splashed her hand in the water.

"Hey, you, get over here," Connor said lightly as he rang the doorbell.

Val immediately listened and ran back by his side. Katie rolled her eyes at how easily her daughter had obeyed Connor. "You do know if I was the one to tell her that, she would still be over there playing in the water and testing my patience."

A sexy grin curved those sinful lips of his. "What can I say? Girls just can't resist the Prescott charm." He winked at her before opening the door and stepping into the house.

Truth, Katie thought, because she was equally guilty of giving in to Connor's many demands in the bedroom. *Give me your mouth* . . . and she did. *Come for me* . . . and her body succumbed. *Ride my cock* . . . and she eagerly complied. Anything he asked for, she didn't hesitate to give, knowing her acquiescence would ultimately be rewarded with the most exquisite pleasure.

"Mom, we're here!" Connor called out in the foyer, jarring her out of her inappropriate thoughts, thank God. As it was, her face was a little warm and no doubt her cheeks were pink.

At the first sound of unfamiliar voices, Val clamped on to Katie's leg, all her original excitement and bravado now reverting to shyness and uncertainty—just as she'd been with Connor that first day he'd met her. Four new faces came out to greet them, all friendly and welcoming and pleased to meet Katie as Connor introduced his parents, then his very pregnant sister, Natalie, and brother-in-law, Wes.

Allison, Connor's mother, bent a little lower to smile at Val, who had her face half-buried in Katie's skirts, clearly overwhelmed by everyone. "You sure are a pretty little girl. And who is that

that you brought with you?" she asked of the unicorn plushy clutched in one of Val's arms.

"Sparkles," Val said softly, tentatively.

"Well, I was just frosting a cake in the kitchen for dessert. Do you think you and Sparkles would like to help?"

That definitely piqued Val's attention and won her over. Katie felt her daughter loosen her hold on her dress, and then she looked up at Connor with those matching blue eyes, as if silently looking to him for his approval.

He held his hand out to her. "Come on, princess. Let's go help your grandma frost a cake. I bet she'll even let you lick the spoon when you're done."

"Easy on the sugar, please," Katie said humorously, because the last thing she wanted was Val bouncing off the walls on their first visit.

Everybody headed toward the kitchen, and Katie glanced at Connor's sister, Natalie, to make conversation about her pregnancy, but she was startled by the tears she saw in the other woman's eyes. "Are you okay?" Katie asked, unsure what had caused the bout of emotion.

"I'm sorry," Natalie said, her expression sentimental. "I seem to be crying over everything lately. It's probably pregnancy hormones, but oh, my God, she is so beautiful and I can't believe I have a niece."

Katie smiled, already liking Natalie. "Thank you. Connor says she looks a lot like you when you were a little girl."

"I see Connor in her, too," Natalie said, blinking away the excess moisture in her eyes. "And you, as well."

As Connor had said, Val was a great combination of both of them. "I brought pictures so you can see her in different stages since she was born."

Natalie placed a hand on her baby bump. "I can't wait to see them."

They were the last two to enter the kitchen, and Val was already kneeling on a stool with a butter knife in her hand, ready to smear frosting on the cake that was on the counter. Connor was right beside her, prepared to intervene if needed, but Allison was telling Val to have fun and giving the little girl carte blanche, and Val was already putting big dollops of chocolate frosting on the cake.

"Do we get to eat it?" Val asked hopefully.

"After you have your dinner," Connor said, totally in dad mode.

"Okay."

Allison smiled at Katie. "Connor said you brought Val's photo album?"

She heard the excitement in the older woman's voice, and Katie nodded and lifted the book she'd carried in the crook of her arm. "Yes."

"Let's sit down at the table," Allison suggested, waving a hand toward the large dining set in the adjoining room. "I'm sure Connor can handle the cake frosting, and we have some time before I send the boys out to barbeque the chicken for dinner, and a hot dog for Val," she added.

"You didn't have to make her anything special."

"I wouldn't expect a three-year-old to eat grilled chicken, scalloped potatoes, and broccoli casserole," Allison said with a laugh. "I can still remember how picky Natalie and Connor were at that age. Would you like something to drink? Sweet tea or a glass of wine?"

"A sweet tea would be lovely," Katie said.

"Me, too, mom," Natalie added.

"You got it. Don't start without me."

When Allison was gone, Natalie leaned back in the chair next to Katie, regarding her with kind but curious eyes before she spoke. "I know we just met, but I have to say that I don't think I've ever seen Connor this happy. I mean, he's always been an easygoing guy, but seeing him now, when he talks about Val, you can see he's a totally different person."

Katie absently traced her finger along the edge of the photo album on the table, allowing herself to open up to Connor's sister. "I honestly didn't know what to expect when I contacted him, considering Val was a complete surprise. A lot of guys might not have been happy having a kid they knew nothing about, but he's been so great with her. I couldn't have asked for a better dad for Val."

"Connor is definitely a stand up kind of guy." Natalie rubbed the top of her belly, as if soothing the baby inside. "But I can assure you, the time he spends with Val isn't out of obligation or a sense of responsibility. It's because she's changed his life, and his future, and Connor is an *all-in* kind of guy. He'll always be there for her."

"I know," Katie said, not doubting his commitment when it came to Val.

Natalie smiled at her. "And just for the record, he talks very fondly of you, too."

"That's sweet," she murmured, not about to get into a serious conversation about her relationship, such as it was, with Connor.

"Here you girls go," Allison said, returning with two glasses of sweet tea. She set them on the table, then sat down so that Katie was the one in the middle of the two women.

They spent the next hour going through the pictures, with Katie giving them a commentary of each one, while Allison and Natalie asked questions about Val's birth and the years and milestones leading up to her third birthday. By the time they were done, she felt the beginnings of a friendship with both women.

In fact, Connor's entire family was gracious and accepting, and by the time they were finished with dinner—which had been full of interesting and amusing facts about Connor's childhood thanks to his father—it felt like she was part of the family. Except . . . she wasn't. She reminded herself that she was there as a default, because she was Val's mom, and while the Prescotts had done nothing to make her feel excluded, a part of her felt as though she was on the outside looking in, and she knew better than to get too attached to something that she'd never had in the first place.

After their meal, and Val's frosted cake for dessert, everyone gathered in the living room for a little bit, the conversation still flowing . . . until Natalie let out a startled gasp.

"Everything okay, Nat?" Wes, her husband, asked, concern etched all over his expression.

"I'm fine," she assured him. "The little guy in my belly sure does have a strong kick and it took me off guard," she said with a laugh. "He's been really active the past few days."

Val, who'd been playing on the floor with her unicorn, jumped up and went to Natalie, her curious gaze taking in her big baby bump. "There's a baby in there?" she asked guilelessly.

"Yes." Natalie smiled. "Do you want to feel him kick?"

Val nodded eagerly, and Natalie took her hand and placed it on the side of her stomach. "Be patient and wait. He's a little stubborn sometimes, like his daddy."

Everyone in the room laughed and gave Wes a hard time, clearly agreeing with Natalie's assessment, while Val remained completely still, her palm pressed to Natalie's belly.

Then, she let out a tiny squeal of surprise and delight. "I felt it!"

Another round of laughter ensued, everybody enjoying Val's innocent and excited reaction.

"When is it coming out?" she asked, blinking up at Natalie.

"Hopefully *very* soon."

Val gently rubbed where the baby had kicked as she patiently waited for more movement. "Can I play with it when it's out?"

"Not right away because he'll be too little," Natalie said. "But when he gets older, I hope you two play together a lot because he'll be your cousin."

"Oh." Val's expression was sweet and naïve, because she wasn't old enough yet to understand what having a cousin meant.

But she would soon enough, because going forward, visits with these good-hearted people would be her new normal. Grandparents, an aunt and an uncle, and cousins—all the things that Katie had never known. Val would be here for holidays and get-togethers, and she'd be a part of a family who wanted her. She'd know security and stability and she'd be loved unconditionally, and for that Katie was grateful.

WITH VAL ASLEEP in her car seat because it was

past her bedtime and Katie staring quietly out the passenger window as Connor drove back to her place, he was all too aware that something was up with the woman sitting next to him.

He'd kept an eye on her during the course of the evening as she'd interacted with his family, to make sure that she was comfortable at all times. She'd hit it off with his sister and his mother, and even his dad had taken a liking to Katie. They'd all talked easily, there had been no awkward moments, and he'd *thought* she'd enjoyed herself, but now he wasn't so sure because her current body language told a different story.

Whatever was on her mind, he didn't want to discuss in the car, only to get cut off when they arrived home. So, instead he turned up the volume on the radio a few notches to fill the silence, so hopefully she'd relax. A little while later, he parked her car in the driveway and turned to her.

"If you'll go open the front door, I'll carry Val in and put her to bed," he told Katie. No sense waking the child and having a cranky kid on their hands.

"Okay," she said, and after getting out of the vehicle, she headed up the walkway.

It didn't take him long to get Val out of her car seat, and as soon as he had her in his arms, she cuddled against his chest so sweetly, so trustingly. Ahhh, if only her mother would let down her walls so easily. Connor was trying to be patient with Katie, to give her time to open up to him and come around to something more than this current arrangement they had, which was part-time co-parenting for him and sex for them. *Great* sex, but still, the fact that he had to leave her bed before Val woke up in the morning told him that she clearly wasn't ready to have him in all aspects of her life. And that's what he ultimately wanted with her . . . because he not only loved Val but he knew without a doubt he loved Katie, as well.

The emotion didn't surprise him. After three and a half years of constantly thinking about her and their one night together, he'd known the moment he'd seen her again a couple of weeks ago that he still had incredibly strong feelings for her. Seeing what an amazing mother she was to their daughter, and getting to know Katie as a person with all her strengths and heartbreaking vulnerabilities, he knew he wanted to be that person for her, the one she could always depend on to be there for her, for the good, the bad, and everything in between.

For him, Katie and Val were a package deal, and building a life with them was what he saw as his future. That's just the kind of guy he was. Casual relationships had never been his thing, and he didn't do things halfway. He wouldn't start now.

He carried Val into the house and to her bedroom. Katie helped get her undressed and into her nightgown, and with Sparkles hugged tight to her chest, Val fell right back into a deep sleep again.

"I'll be in the kitchen making a cup of hot tea," Katie said in a soft voice while Connor finished tucking in Val. "Would you like anything?"

He shook his head. "No, I'm good. I'll be there in a sec."

Katie left the room, and Connor watched his daughter for a few extra seconds while brushing his fingers along her soft, chubby cheek. She was absolutely perfect, an angel who made him want to be a better man for her, and the best dad possible. From the moment he'd found out about her, she'd changed his life, and for the better.

In his eyes, there was a reason Val was conceived when the odds had been so highly stacked against the possibility. She was meant to be, and her existence had brought her mother back to him, giving them the second chance they both deserved.

Convincing Katie of that was proving to be much more difficult.

With a sigh, he left Val's room and closed the door behind him. He found Katie in the kitchen, swirling a tea bag in a steaming mug of hot water. She had to have heard him enter the room, yet she didn't turn around, keeping as silent and brooding as she'd been on the way home. He got the impression that she wanted to be alone, but unless she blatantly told him to leave, he wasn't going anywhere. Not until he knew what had put her in this funk in the first place. They'd made headway over the past couple of weeks, but it felt like whatever had set her off today had pushed them two giant steps *back*, instead of forward like he'd hoped.

"You were awfully quiet on the drive home," he said, leaning against the counter across from where she was standing to give her space. "I hope you had a nice time?"

"I did. Your family is wonderful," she said as she squeezed the excess moisture from her tea bag into her mug. "It makes me realize how dysfunctional mine always was."

Ahhh, now they were getting somewhere. This was the one area she'd always been vague about. He knew her parents were divorced, that she was an only child, and she wasn't close to either parent now. What he didn't know was how that family dynamic had affected her, personally, as a kid. He had a feeling that a lot of her insecurities stemmed from that time in her life.

"I'd really like to hear about what happened with yours," he said, keeping his voice neutral.

Stirring honey into her tea, she gave her head a hard shake as she glanced over her shoulder at him. "Trust me, you really don't."

The corner of his mouth hitched up in a smile. "Trust *me*, Katie, I really *do* want to know, or I wouldn't have asked."

Setting her spoon in the sink, she picked up her mug and turned around, leaning against the counter across from where he stood. She seemed to consider whether or not to go down this route before she finally spoke. "In a nut-shell, my childhood, and what I had of a family, was the complete opposite of yours. My mother got pregnant, and my father married her out of obligation, not love, so no big surprise that they got divorced."

He heard the pain and resentment in her voice, and while his first instinct was to get rid of the distance between them so he could comfort her, he remained right where he was. He knew there was a lot more to her story, so he waited while she took a sip of her tea, then continued.

"So, I was four at the time they split up, and it was nasty. Even at that young age, I remember lots of fighting and arguments and each of them doing and saying things to hurt the other, and quite honestly, in all my eighteen years of being raised by them, that never stopped." She paused for a moment and wrapped her hands around her coffee mug, and he didn't miss the hurt, even so many years later, that filtered through her dark brown eyes. "There were constant custody battles with me in the middle, and when I was a bit older, I realized that even though my parents went to court to fight over me, it wasn't because they *wanted* me. I was a pawn between them, used as leverage to hold something over the other person. And it didn't matter how good I was or how I desperately tried to please either of them, it didn't make a difference. It wasn't about me, it was about them and what they wanted. I was just a casualty of their failed marriage."

He swore beneath his breath and crossed his arms over his chest, wishing he could erase those horrible memories from her mind. But he couldn't. Those emotional scars clearly colored how she viewed their arrangement with Val, and why she was so cautious and guarded. Especially since both Katie and her mother had gotten pregnant unexpectedly. He didn't have to be a rocket scientist to realize that Katie kept her heart under wraps because she didn't want to risk their daughter getting caught up in a similar custody situation. And it didn't help matters that the last guy she'd been in a relationship with had totally fucked her over.

"So, yeah, my family situation has always been pretty screwed up . . . but I'm really glad that Val will have grandparents who will love her. At least your side of the family will never make her feel like she's not wanted."

Her voice was so thick with emotion, and he couldn't stay away from her any longer. Pushing away from the counter, he crossed the kitchen to her, then took her mug from her hands and put it on the surface behind her. Then he gently pulled her against him, embracing her, silently comforting her. He couldn't change her past or her childhood, but he could show her that things could be different. That *he* was different—from her father and all the men that came after him.

But for now, he just wanted her to feel cared for and loved . . . even though he knew she wasn't ready to hear those words from him. Verbally, he held them back, but he'd show her how much she meant to him in other ways.

"Put your arms around me, sweetheart," he said when she hadn't fully relaxed against him and was relieved when she did as he requested. "I want you to know what it feels like to hold on to me, to know that I'm here for you, that you matter to me and I would never deliberately hurt you." She just needed to believe it.

After a while, he released her and took her hand in his. "Come on, I'm going to put you to bed," he said with a gentle smile, no sexual overtures involved, because that's not what she needed tonight.

He led her back to her bedroom and made her put on her comfy tank top and pajama shorts while he stripped down to his briefs. After turning off the light, he got beneath the covers with her and pulled her close, spooning against her backside. He'd only snuggle with her for a little while, because he knew that him staying the night still wasn't an option for Katie.

When he slid his hand around her waist, she grabbed his arm and pulled it tight around her, silently needing him—even if she wasn't ready to say the words.

"Go to sleep, sweetheart," he murmured against her ear. "I got you."

And he knew he always would.

Chapter Eleven

"MOMMY, YOU LOOK so pretty!"

Katie smiled at her daughter, who was looking up at her with wide eyes filled with little-girl wonder. "Thank you, sweetie pie," she said as she put on a pair of dangling crystal-cut earrings.

As Katie looked in her dresser mirror, she had to admit that she *did* look pretty... and sexy. Since having Val, she'd never had a reason to own a little black dress, or anything fancier than a casual one. So, when Connor had insisted on taking her out to a nice dinner to celebrate the new contract she'd just signed to handle all the logos and branding for a chain of restaurants, she'd gone out and splurged on herself.

The dress was formfitting to her curves and long-sleeved since the evenings were getting much cooler as they headed into fall. But it was the deep vee neckline that had sold Katie, because it showcased her breasts in a subtle but eye-catching way . . . which meant she'd also had to buy a new, lacy push-up bra and matching panties. Her strappy heels had a sparkle of rhinestones, and she'd given her hair some extra volume and gone with a soft, charcoal eye shadow to accentuate her eyes.

"Where are you going?" Val asked as she climbed up onto Katie's bed.

"Out to dinner." After pulling out the tube of pale pink lipstick she'd bought at the department store, Katie smoothed a layer on her lips.

"With Daddy?"

Katie smiled at her daughter in the mirror as she spritzed on a light mist of perfume. "Yes."

"Can I come with you?" she asked hopefully.

"No, honey, it's for adults only." It was also the first time in the six weeks that they'd been in this arrangement that she and Connor had gone out together without Val. "Melissa is coming over to watch you for a few hours and to put you to bed, so be good for her, okay?" Katie said of the college-aged girl who lived across the street that she and Leah used occasionally for babysitting.

Val gave a little pout. "Okay."

"Hey, tomorrow is Monday and you've got school in the morning, so you need to be bright-eyed and bushy-tailed."

The doorbell rang and Val's sullen mood instantly transformed into excitement. "Daddy!" she shouted as she scrambled off the bed and ran to the front room, even though she knew she couldn't open the door until Katie got there.

Katie was about ten seconds behind her daughter, and she couldn't deny that she felt a little nervous about Connor's reaction when he saw her, when all he'd ever seen her in was mom clothes. "Did you ask who it is?"

"Yes, and it's *Daddy*," Val said with an exaggerated roll of her eyes. "I told you so."

Katie checked the peephole just to be sure and felt a dozen flutters in her stomach when she saw his gorgeous face and those stunning blue eyes staring back at her. She would have thought after all these weeks that the giddiness would subside, just like it always had in the past with other men, but it was still alive and strong.

"Okay, you can open the door."

Val flung the door wide and literally jumped up into Connor's arms, which he was totally ready for since that's how the little girl always greeted him. One strong arm bolstered her up by the bottom as Val gave him a big hug. Seeing her daughter's enthusiastic reaction to Connor never got old, either.

"How's my girl?" he asked, his focus and attention one hundred percent on Val as he walked into the house with her still in his arms.

"I'm good!" she said in an animated voice, and then she frowned. "But I missed you today."

Usually on Sundays Connor spent at least the afternoon with Val, but he'd called that morning to tell the little girl that he had some things he needed to take care of. Val had moped around for the better part of the day because her attachment to Connor had grown that strong.

"I know. I missed you, too, princess," Connor said as he set her down on her feet. "But I promise to come by for dinner tomorrow night, and we can play Candyland, okay?"

"Okay," Val said, then tugged on his hand.

"Doesn't Mommy look pretty?"

Connor had been so focused on Val that he hadn't seen her yet. But he looked now, and by the time his dark, smoldering gaze had traveled down her body, then back up again to her warm, blushing face, Katie felt the need to fan herself.

"Wow, you look . . . " *fucking hot*, he mouthed to her in deference to his daughter's little ears. "Amazing."

She laughed at that last polite word, realizing she much preferred the dirty ones better. "Thank you. You clean up pretty well yourself, Mr. Prescott."

He was wearing a pair of black slacks, a plum-colored shirt, and a black overcoat that made his shoulders look broader and his chest wider. She could have easily used the same *fucking hot* description for him, too.

Katie pulled her phone from her small purse. "Let me give Melissa a call to let her know you're here, and as soon as she arrives, we can leave for our . . . " She'd almost said date, but this *wasn't* a date and she certainly didn't want to define it as one.

"Celebratory dinner?" he offered, his voice as direct as his gaze, as if he knew what had just passed through her mind and was catering to it.

"Yeah," she said, and turned around as she put the phone to her ear as it began to ring, so she didn't have to look him in the eyes, because those deep, endless blue eyes . . . they made her weak, and the man himself made her want things she knew better than to wish for or count on.

Melissa picked up after several rings, and Katie said, "We're ready to go."

The girl promised to be right over, and when Katie glanced back at Connor, she was relieved to find his attention on Val. She had to admit, things were good right now with Connor. Very status quo. She liked their uncomplicated routine, as well as the fact that she knew what to expect on a day-to-day basis. Regular visits from Connor, dinners together, him now mowing her lawn, watching him bond with Val, and at night . . . well, there was nothing *routine* about the way he fucked her. Connor definitely wasn't strictly a missionary kind of man, though even when he was, he always managed to make her feel completely and utterly consumed by him.

Everything *outside* of the bedroom felt bal-anced and calm and predictable, just the way she preferred it. She was being practical about the arrangement, and about her affair with Connor. She tried her best not to have any expectations other than what they'd already established, knowing it was the easiest way to avoid heartbreak when all the shiny newness wore off and Connor moved on.

Melissa arrived, and after giving Val a kiss, Katie headed out the door and down the walkway, with Connor beside her, his hand resting low on her back. She glanced out to the curb, startled to find a brand-new SUV parked there instead of his utility truck.

"Is that yours?" she asked.

"Yep. That's where I was today, at the dealership buying a car that's going to be much easier to put Val's car seat in." He hit the remote and the locks disengaged so he could open the passenger-side door for her. "Thought it would be fun for us to take it for a test spin tonight."

She slid into the leather seat, impressed by the brand-new, no-expense-spared vehicle. He'd never had to take Val out by himself, because right now they did everything together, but she knew that time would come and she was glad he was thinking ahead.

She had no idea where he'd planned on taking her, and she had to admit that she was impressed when they ended up on the fortieth floor of the Chicago Stock Exchange building and had reservations at the exclusive Everest restaurant. Connor had managed to secure a window seat, and the view of Chicago's skyline at night was breathtaking.

He chose a bottle of expensive champagne, and after they ordered their meals, he toasted to her new contract. They talked about his work and the projects he was currently working on, and how Wes and his other partner, Max, were dealing with the fact that they'd recently become fathers. She, Val, and Connor had gone to Wes and Natalie's a few days after the birth of their baby boy, Dylan, so Val could meet her new cousin.

Katie had brought a gift, and when Natalie had insisted that she hold the baby while she opened the present, Katie had been overwhelmed with emotion as she remembered those early days with Val, when she was little and cuddly and so precious. But seeing little Dylan in Connor's big, strong arms had brought a pang to Katie's heart, as did the sweet way Val talked to the baby and gently touched his tiny fingers and hand.

"It cracks me up how bleary-eyed both Wes and Max look when they come into the office in the morning because of their babies being up at all hours of the night," Connor said in amusement. "And soon, Kyle is going to be in the same position when Ella has her baby."

"It's definitely an adjustment," Katie said as she finished her second glass of champagne, then looked at Connor seated across from her, their only lighting coming from the candle on their table. He might have told her it was a celebratory dinner, but the whole atmosphere was undeniably romantic and intimate . . . like a date.

He was smiling at her, looking relaxed and so handsome, and she just wanted to enjoy the night and not overthink things. They'd already eaten a delicious dinner, and they'd both declined dessert, and once the waiter cleared their dishes away, Connor poured the last of the champagne into her glass for her to finish.

She raised a brow at him. "Are you trying to get me drunk so you can take advantage of me?" she teased.

"Are you?" he asked with a light, husky laugh that made her breasts ache and her nipples grow tight. "Getting drunk?"

"No." She licked the taste of the champagne from her bottom lip, nearly groaning when his gaze zeroed in on her mouth. "I just feel good, though I certainly drank most of that bottle."

"I'm good to drive, so enjoy it. Tonight is all about you, because you deserve to be spoiled." Then he gave her a wicked grin that made her shift restlessly in her chair. "And if you think that this dinner was amazing, wait until we get home and have dessert. I can't wait to eat mine," he murmured meaningfully.

The sexual innuendo in his words had heat and lust and so much *need* swirling through her. "I think I'm ready to go and have dessert now."

"Me, too," he said, just as anxiously.

He paid the bill, and fifteen minutes later, they were in his SUV and heading back to her house for dessert.

THE SEXUAL TENSION and heightened desire filling the close confines of the vehicle were nearly tangible on the ride to Katie's. Every time Connor inhaled, he caught the fragrance of her perfume . . . and the richer scent of her arousal, and it didn't help matters that she kept shifting in her seat and rubbing her legs restlessly together.

He honest to God didn't mean for their evening to take such a quick leap to sexy times, but he supposed it was his own fault for making the suggestive comment about dessert. He always wanted Katie, that was a given, but tonight was supposed to be about wining and dining her, and romance, and them as a couple—despite her attempts at keeping their outing as a celebratory dinner, rather than considering it the date he'd intended it to be.

After six weeks of being in her life, he was no longer satisfied with pretending they weren't a couple during the day, then having hot, mind-blowing sex at night—only for him to go home afterwards instead of staying until morning like two normal, consenting adults would agree to. Her excuse was always Val . . . but that's all it was. Just an excuse to protect *her* emotions, not her daughter's.

He was beyond ready to take that next step with Katie, the one that enabled them to build what they currently had into something deeper and infinitely more stable. Whether she wanted to believe it or not, they were already in a relationship . . . but now he wanted the commitment to go with it, along with the freedom to be openly affectionate with her and not have to hold back on PDAs in front of Val, or anyone else for that matter. He'd done everything possible to prove that he was a man she could rely on, that being a father to Val was his first priority, and that he was the kind of guy who wanted the whole package . . . with her and Val.

Tonight, he intended to tell Katie how he felt about her. He knew she cared about him. Hell, he'd like to believe she was even falling in love with him. But now knowing about her family history, and the men who had come before him, he had a feeling that finding a way past her walls and defenses was going to be like attempting to tear down the Berlin Wall. Difficult, with a whole lot of resistance.

But he was willing to try, because Katie was worth it.

"Are we almost there yet?" she asked in a low, sultry voice that made him grin, because it matched their daughter's impatience when they were going places.

He glanced at her, groaning at the way she was biting her lower lip, and watching as her fingers trailed down the perfect vee of her neckline that teased him with the plump curves of her breasts. "Soon," he said through gritted teeth.

He returned his gaze to the road, maintaining a tight grip on the steering wheel to try and keep his hands to himself until they were alone in her bedroom, but when she reached out and grabbed his hand, then brought it over to her side and placed it very high on her thigh, his good behavior evaporated.

Connor didn't know if it was the champagne that was making her so brazen, but did it really matter when he was more than willing to indulge her in whatever game she was playing? When she guided his flattened palm beneath the hem of her dress, then all the way up to that sweet spot between her legs, it was all he could do to concentrate on the drive home. She pressed his fingers against her sex and rubbed them along the soft, swollen flesh he could feel through her soaked panties.

She shuddered when he came in contact with her clit and massaged a little harder, a little faster, through the wet silk. "Connor," she panted as her head fell back against the seat, her legs open wide and her hips pushing shamelessly against his fingers as he played with her.

"Don't stop . . . please don't stop," she begged.

Somehow, when they arrived at her place, he managed to maneuver the car to the curb, but he had no choice but to retrieve his hand to shut off the engine. As soon as he severed contact, she made a frustrated sound in the back of her throat, clearly a little miffed that he'd brought her to the edge but hadn't pushed her all the way over the peak.

"That was cruel," she complained with a sultry pout. "I was so close."

He gave her a hot, seductive smile. "You're not coming until I'm buried so deep inside of you all I can feel is you wrapped completely around my cock." Until she felt every part of him become a part of her . . . heart, body, and soul.

She released a soft moan. "Then let's hurry, because I want that, too."

His dick was throbbing inside his pants, totally on board with her suggestion, but as he looked into those big brown eyes, he realized that he wanted tonight to be different. That instead of a fast, hard fuck, he wanted to make love to Katie . . . with her knowing exactly how he felt about her.

He reached out and tenderly feathered the backs of his fingers along her warm cheek—a touch that was deliberately intimate but not sexual. "Katie . . . there's something I need to tell you," he said, and immediately saw a flash of uncertainty eclipse the desire in her gaze, because she was smart enough to guess what he wanted to say.

And she wasn't ready to hear it, because she hastily shook her head in denial. "I don't want to talk right now, Connor," she said, her voice holding a desperate quality to it. "Please."

He debated whether or not to say the words anyway, to get them out in the open, where they belonged, but with Katie suddenly in fight-or-flight mode, he decided it wasn't a discussion he wanted to have in his car. That it would be better to have inside the house once the babysitter was gone.

He didn't say anything more as they both got out of the vehicle and he walked with her up to the front porch. Once inside the house, Melissa assured them that Val had been great and was sound asleep in bed. Connor paid the young girl generously, then walked her outside and made sure she made it to her place across the street safely, before returning to Katie, who was waiting for him in the living room.

As soon as he closed and locked the front door, she was pushing him a few steps back while shoving his jacket off his shoulders, her mouth open and hot on his. No, she clearly did *not* want to talk, and was using sex as a diversion.

Somehow, he found himself backed up against the nearest wall, her hands working frantically to unbuckle his belt to free his thick, aching cock. Passion and lust had never been an issue for them, but there was a palpable urgency to her seduction that had never been there before, and the fact that she was ready and willing to strip him naked where Val might catch them told him how intent she was on avoiding any conversation.

As her fingers curled around his cock and she began stroking him in a tight fist, Connor realized he had two choices. Let this continue where it was heading, toward a fast, mindless fuck so she didn't have to think, or take control of the situation and make love to her on *his* terms, not hers. He opted for the latter, because one way or another, this night was going to end with Katie knowing exactly how he felt about her—and with him in charge.

He pulled his mouth from hers, and she made a small sound of distress in the back of her throat as he ended the kiss. "We need to take this into the bedroom," he said huskily, and her gaze cleared just enough to give him a nod of understanding.

He led the way, and as soon as the door was closed behind them, they were stripping out of their clothes. As he watched, her dress fell to the floor, and lust seared through him when he saw what she wore beneath . . . tiny black lace panties and a matching bra that pushed her breasts up like an offering. Normally, he'd take the time to slowly strip away the sexy lingerie and savor everything it revealed, but she didn't want slow and seductive, as was evident in the way she was already unhooking her bra, then shoving her underwear down her legs.

Completely naked, she laid back on the bed, and he was right behind her, his clothes strewn on the ground as he rolled on a condom and joined her. Without any preliminaries, because he'd already felt how ready she was for him out in the car, he entered her in one fluid thrust that had her moaning in extreme pleasure. Eyes closed, she arched her back, wound her legs around his waist, and grabbed at his ass, urging him to take her harder, faster, deeper.

He deliberately did the opposite and slowed down, grinding against her clit every time he pushed into her with just enough control to keep her on the edge. She writhed eagerly beneath him, desperately trying to quicken his pace, but he pinned her body more securely to the bed, restricting her movements until he was ready to let her come.

Her lashes fluttered back open, her dark, sultry eyes searching his. "I need you, Connor . . . *please*," she whispered, so much passion in her voice.

With his forearms braced on the bed beside her, he buried his hands into her hair, tangling it around his fingers and forcing her head back so her gaze remained locked on his. "I want more than your *need*," he said, his tone rough around the edges. "I want your love, Katie."

Panic flared across her expression, and she tried to shake her head in denial. "Connor . . . "

"I love you," he told her before she could refute his claim. "I just wanted and needed you to know that."

Her eyes were wide, and knowing she needed time to process his declaration, he drove back into her, finally allowing her body the pleasure it sought and giving her mind something else to focus on. Another demanding thrust, and she moaned at the depth and fullness of his shaft impaling her to the hilt. Again and again, he claimed her, until she started to climax and took him along for the overwhelmingly intense ride.

Over the next few hours, he didn't give her time to think or obsess or worry about the words he'd spoken to her. Instead, he showed her how much he cared and how much she meant to him, in the way he thoroughly worshiped her body, until she was so exhausted she fell into a deep sleep in his arms.

He held her close, knowing he'd have to leave soon, and told himself that tomorrow would be soon enough to figure out where to go from here.

Chapter Twelve

"**M**OMMY," A SOFT, girlish voice whispered, weaving through Katie's mind and tugging at her subconscious.

"Mommy, wake up," the sound came again, this time with a gentle pat to Katie's cheek that definitely roused her.

She blinked her eyes open and stared at her daughter, who was standing at the side of her bed. Going by the light coming in from the bedroom windows, it was morning, and judging by the heavy, masculine arm draped around her waist and the hard length of an erection prodding against her ass, Connor was still in her bed, his warm body spooned behind hers.

Crap! He'd stayed the night, and clearly they hadn't locked the door.

A jolt of panic had Katie scrambling up in her bed, which proved to be an unwise idea since she was still naked beneath the blankets. She pulled the sheet up to make sure she stayed covered from her chest down, and her quick movements jostled Connor awake, too. She heard him release a soft, *oh, shit*, beneath his breath, and much more carefully, he sat up beside her, being equally strategic with the covers around his hips.

"Hey, sweetie pie," Katie said in a cheerful voice that sounded forced to her own ears. "What are you doing up so early?" It really wasn't early. A glance at her cell phone on the night stand showed it was 7:28 a.m., and her daughter was due to leave for preschool in half an hour.

"I woke up all by myself," she said, then glanced at Connor curiously. "Why are you in Mommy's bed?" she asked, her tone guileless. "Did you have a bad dream? Mommy only lets me stay in here when I have a bad dream."

Thank God for a child's naiveté, Katie thought, grateful that Val's mind went to such an innocent scenario.

"Yes, princess," he said, striving for a light tone even though his voice was still gruff from sleep. "I did have a bad dream."

"Oh." She leaned her little arms against the mattress, seemingly in no hurry to go anywhere, and continued her chatter. "Did Mommy kiss away your fears and hug you to keep you safe from the monsters like she does for me?"

An abrupt chuckle escaped Connor from behind Katie, but she wasn't as amused and needed to divert Val's attention, and quickly. "Honey, why don't you go and get dressed for school, and I'll meet you in the kitchen for breakfast in a few minutes."

"Okay." Val skipped from the room, and as soon as she was gone, Katie jump out of bed and closed and locked the door.

Grabbing a pair of underwear from her dresser, she pulled them on, and continued with a bra, jeans, and a T-shirt before turning back to Connor, who was now sitting on the edge of the bed with the sheet still draped around his hips.

"This shouldn't have happened," she said, unable to keep the edge of anger from her voice. "*How* did this happen?"

He scrubbed a hand along the stubble covering his jaw, then pushed those long fingers through his already disheveled hair. "We both fell asleep. It's not that big of a deal, Katie," he said, trying to placate her.

She stiffened defensively. "Yes, it *is* a big deal. It's misleading and confusing for Val."

He met her gaze and held it steadily. "Then maybe it's time for us to renegotiate our arrangement."

He was completely serious, and her heart pounded hard and heavy in her chest, because she wasn't sure she could give him what he was asking for—something far more serious than an affair. The kind of commitment that she was afraid to believe in because, in the past, it always ended in pain and misery for her.

She pulled in a deep breath as everything that had happened last night came flooding back in an overwhelming wave of emotion—mainly, the honest, candid way he'd confessed his love for her. That same sentiment shone in his deep blue eyes, promising her so much if she would just take a chance and trust him.

Except her deep-seated fear of rejection, the same one that had colored her childhood and had carried over into her adult relationships, kept her from giving him what he wanted, what he deserved. For her, love never lasted, and the men who'd come and gone through her life always grew bored and moved on. That was all she knew, and it was just a matter of time before Connor did the same.

A huge, aching lump formed in her throat. The two of them had clearly come to that crossroads, where she was now forced to decide which direction to choose when it came to her and Connor . . . and for her daughter's sake. To keep things amicable between them, Katie knew it was time to let him go as a lover, in order to keep him as a friend.

CONNOR STARED AT his reflection in the bathroom mirror, a sense of dread balling in his stomach. He didn't have to be a genius to realize that Katie had just done a one-eighty on him out in the bedroom. That having Val find the two of them in bed together had all her doubts and insecurities about them rushing to the surface.

He'd known they'd get to this point eventually, where Katie would have to make some difficult decisions about their relationship. He didn't want to be the guy who fucked her when the mood struck. He wanted to be the man who loved her, took care of her, and was a part of her life on a daily basis, twenty-four seven.

He'd given her six weeks to come around, while doing his best to prove to her that he wasn't like every other guy in her past, that their relationship wasn't a replica of her parents'. Today was the day he'd find out if any of his efforts had paid off, because he couldn't continue with this part-time arrangement with Katie and she was going to have to make a choice—all of him or nothing at all. His stomach twisted at the latter thought, which was a very real possibility.

He splashed water on his face and dried it with a towel, then walked back into Katie's bedroom to get dressed. She was already out in the kitchen with Val, and he joined them as soon as he was fully clothed. He knew Katie heard him walk over to the coffeepot on the counter and pour himself a cup, but she didn't look at him as she made Val a peanut butter and jelly sandwich for her lunch.

Connor sat down next to his daughter at the table, who was eating her bowl of cereal. After taking a bite of her breakfast, she scooped up more of the Honey Nut Cheerios and held it toward him.

"Want some of my O's, Daddy?" she asked,

cheerful, bright-eyed, and completely unaware of the tension between the two adults in the room. "Or some of my juice?"

He smiled at her. "I'm good, princess. You need to eat all that yourself so you go to school with a full belly."

She set her spoon in her bowl, then lifted her shirt and pushed out her stomach with an adorable grin. "I already have a full belly!"

"Looks like we need to make more room for your breakfast then," he teased, and gently poked a finger against her midsection, which made her suck her tummy back in and giggle.

"I like you being here for breakfast," she said happily as she picked up her glass of orange juice. "I want you here *every* morning."

God, he wanted that, too. So much. But the tense set of Katie's shoulders said otherwise, and instead of answering—because he had no idea how the next hour or so was going to shake out between him and Katie—he took a drink of his coffee instead.

Val finished eating, and after taking her dishes to the counter by the sink, she came back and lifted her My Little Pony backpack from the rung on the back of her chair and slipped her arms through the straps. Once that was done, she leaned against Connor's leg and looked up at him with hopeful eyes.

"Will you take me to school today?" she asked, so sweetly his heart squeezed tight in his chest, because it was such a natural thing for him to do . . . if they'd been a family.

Before he could respond, Katie was next to Val and replied for him. "Daddy has to go to work," she said, tucking her lunch into the little girl's backpack, her voice strained. "So I'm going to take you and Leah."

Val pouted. "But I want Daddy to take me since he's here."

Connor wasn't going to contradict Katie or undermine her decision. He would never instigate a power struggle with Val in the middle, no matter what happened between the two of them. However, he hated how confused Val seemed to be, that Connor was there, yet he wasn't able to do something as simple as drop her off at school.

He set his coffee mug on the table. "Come here, princess," he said, and when his daughter was close enough, he lifted her so that she was sitting on his lap, a hint of sadness in her big blue eyes. "I have to go to work, but I'll see you tonight, okay?" He'd *always* be there for Val.

That would never change no matter what his relationship with her mother ended up being.

"Okay," she said, but not happily.

He tapped Val on her cute nose, which he knew would make her grin, and it did. "And if you're good for your mommy today, I'll take you out for ice cream after you eat your dinner." With or without Katie joining them remained to be seen.

She clapped her hands gleefully. "I want chocolate chip!"

"You got it." He set Val back on her feet and watched as Katie grabbed her purse and car keys from the counter.

For the first time since bolting out of the bedroom before they could really talk, she finally glanced at him and met his gaze. The fear he'd seen earlier in her eyes had abated to a silent conviction, and he had no doubts that she'd already reinforced all those emotional walls that he'd spent the past six weeks trying to tear down.

"You can lock the door when you leave," she said, her voice tight, as if she was trying really hard to keep her shit together until she was alone.

He didn't say anything as she followed Val

out the front door, because he wasn't planning on going anywhere until she came back and he had his say, which she hadn't yet given him the chance to do.

He spent the next twenty minutes making a few phones calls, one of which was to his partner, Kyle, whom he was supposed to meet at a jobsite this morning to discuss some renovation plans for a house they'd recently purchased. He rescheduled for later that afternoon, and once he'd checked in with one of his project managers who'd already left him a message, Connor went into the living room, sat down on the couch, and waited for Katie to return.

When she walked through the front door, she obviously wasn't surprised to see him, since his SUV was still parked out at the curb. But everything about her was wary—her gaze, her demeanor, and the way she set her purse down on the coffee table but remained standing instead of sitting by him.

"I think you and I have some unresolved issues to settle," he said, jumping right into the fray because, well, there was no easy way to have this conversation.

"There's nothing unresolved, Connor."

He arched a brow and didn't hesitate to call her out. "Do you plan to completely ignore the fact that I told you that I love you?"

He saw a flicker of emotion in her eyes that resembled heartache and regret. "It's not so much that I'm ignoring it . . . I'm really trying to think of Val and do what's best for her."

"And you think that ending our personal relationship is what's best for her?" he asked, unable to keep the incredulous tone from his voice. "Or is it best for *you* because ending things means that there is no risk of *you* getting hurt?"

She visibly stiffened, as if his words had hit their intended target. "It's best for *both* of us," she said, crossing her arms over her chest defensively. "I don't have a great track record when it comes to men, Connor. In fact, they always leave because I either wasn't worth the effort for a long-term relationship or I wasn't enough in some way to keep them interested. Even my own father didn't stick around, unless he needed to use me as some kind of leverage against my mother."

Her chin lifted a few determined notches. "So yes, in that regard, I'm being proactive, because if something happens between you and me and it ends bitterly, that *will* directly affect Val. She'll get caught in the middle, and I refuse to put our daughter through what I endured growing up because my parents grew to hate each other. I . . . I can't take that risk," she said, her voice pained. "You and I are better off just being friends, instead of complicating things with sex and . . . emotions."

Connor exhaled a deep breath, remembering that night after they'd visited his parents for the first time, when Katie had opened up and told him about her childhood—her parents' nasty divorce, the constant custody battles that no young child should ever have to suffer through, and all the rejections that had left her unable to trust in any relationship.

Without a doubt, her emotional scars and insecurities ran deep, and while he understood that in her mind she was truly trying to protect Val, she was doing so at the cost of her own happiness. And all he could do was put everything out in the open between them and reinforce how he felt about her. The rest would have to be up to Katie.

Standing up, he walked over to her, ignoring the way she eyed him so guardedly because there was nothing she could say or do that would change the fact that he loved her. Given the chance, he knew he wanted to marry her, but she wasn't there yet . . . and quite possibly never would be. The realization made him feel as though someone had stabbed him in the chest with a sharp knife and given it an extra twist for good measure.

He uncrossed her arms from where she'd folded them in front of her and took her hands in his. Her brows creased in sudden confusion, because his gentle actions contradicted the heated argument they'd just had. All he had left to give her was the truth, so that's what he did.

He tenderly rubbed his thumbs over the backs of her hands. "When I met you over three and a half years ago in that Denver airport, I saw a vulnerable woman who'd been hurt by some asshole who clearly hadn't appreciated how beautiful you are, inside and out. His loss was my gain, and I was lucky to have that one amazing night with you that I'll never forget, because we created the best thing that has ever happened to me. Our daughter."

She swallowed hard, clearly affected by his words, but remained quiet, so he continued because he didn't need a response from her. He just needed her to hear what was in his heart.

"I thought about you constantly during all those years, because what we had in one night was stronger than anything I've ever felt for any other woman . . . and still is," he said, meaning it. "If my feelings for you can withstand three and a half years of not even being with you physically, and all based on one night together, then you can bet that I'm the kind of guy who can go the distance. I don't give up when things get tough. I believe in love, and I believe in what we have together. I want to fight for you, for us, but you have to give me *something* to fight for."

She shook her head and blinked back the tears he saw forming in her eyes, not giving him what he desperately needed from her—some kind of affirmation, or a kernel of hope that she wanted to at least *try*.

"I want you to be *mine*," he said, not caring how possessive that sounded, because it's exactly how he felt. "I want to go to bed with you at night and wake up with you in the morning, without worrying about sneaking out of the house before Val sees us together. I want us to be a family, Katie, except you're too afraid to take a chance on the real deal, and whether you want to accept it or not, that's what we have. A strong relationship with the potential of being so much more, if you would just trust me with your heart. I promise I won't ever break it."

"Connor . . . I just . . . can't." She tugged her hands from his, and as soon as she severed the connection between them, Connor *knew* there was nothing else he could say to convince her that they were meant to be.

"ARGHH!" KATIE EXHALED the frustrated sound and scrapped the graphic ad she was working on, the fourth version since Connor had picked up Val to take her to see her new baby cousin, who she was completely enamored with—enough that she kept asking for a baby brother of her own and couldn't understand why Katie couldn't just make it happen.

Connor and Val had been gone nearly three hours, and with the house quiet, she'd planned to get caught up on the work that had piled up over the past week and a half since she'd ended her affair with Connor. Since he'd walked out her door after baring his soul and had gotten nothing in return because she'd been too petrified to let go of all her emotional childhood baggage—and some adult issues, too—and be strong and confident and have faith in every promise he'd made.

Since that day, her creativity had been in lock-down. It was as if her mind was rebelling against the rash, short-sighted decision she'd made to push Connor out of her life, and instead was forcing her to think about everything she'd given up and lost.

Well . . . not *lost* yet, her brain taunted her. But she did stand to lose a one-of-a-kind man who been nothing but dependable, loyal, and the kind of father to Val that Katie wished she'd had growing up. Because despite everything he'd said to her that last morning, it wasn't fair to think or believe that he'd wait around for her forever. Not when she hadn't given him any reason to.

The ache in her chest that had been a perpetual reminder of what an idiot she'd been to let him go seemed to increase day by day, as did her doubts and convictions when it came to her reasons for doing so. Every time she saw Connor—which was every day, since he saw Val in the evenings after work and on the weekends—only made her realize how much she missed him. Not the sex, but just being with him, and the three of them doing things together as . . . well, a family.

That no longer happened. In the beginning it had been Katie's choice to opt out of the time Connor spent with Val, even though he'd initially asked her to join them on their outings—because for one thing, it had been too painful to be around Connor, and for another, she'd been trying to establish those boundaries between the two of them and wanted to make the custody arrangement as easy as possible on Val. Except it had only made it more difficult and confusing for the three-year-old little girl, who'd grown used to them being a trio, and now her mother was no longer part of the equation.

Katie understood that confusion, because she was experiencing it herself more and more. Tack on the fact that she missed Connor *so much*, and was it no wonder that she couldn't get a damn thing done, work-wise?

Her doorbell rang, startling her out of her thoughts, and she figured Connor and Val were most likely back from his sister's. Inhaling a deep breath to gather the fortitude to face him for the few minutes it took to drop off their daughter, she headed out to the living room and opened the front door—and found Avery standing there instead.

"Hey," Katie said, surprised to see her friend.

Avery lifted a plate with some kind of decadent confection sitting on top. "I brought you a lemon loaf cake with icing," she said with a grin. "I think you and I need to have a girl talk, and what better way to do that than with dessert?"

Katie had an idea of what kind of "girl talk" Avery was interested in having, and honestly, she was shocked it had taken her friend this long to force the issue of what had happened between Katie and Connor. The first time she'd asked, which had been the day everything had changed between the two of them, Katie hadn't been ready to talk, for fear of having an emotional breakdown over her decision. But enough time had passed that having a conversation about Connor wouldn't reduce her to tears or the sobbing mess she'd been at night when Val was fast asleep in her bed and Katie was all alone.

"Come on in," Katie invited, and the two of them headed into the kitchen. "Would you like coffee or iced tea?"

"Let's go with iced tea," Avery said as she

set the lemon loaf on the counter, then took down two smaller plates from the overhead cupboard.

While Katie filled two glasses with their drink of choice, Avery handled the cutting of the cake. They sat down at the table, and Avery gave her the chance to taste just one bite of the delicious treat before she spoke what was on her mind.

"So, what is it going to take to make you come to your senses about Connor?" she asked, point-blank. "I've spent the past week and a half seeing you depressed and watching that gorgeous guy who clearly adores you looking equally miserable, so clearly, neither one of you is happy just being *friends*."

Katie winced at her friend's blatant, and accurate, depiction of her and Connor. "Yeah, it's been . . . rough."

"That man is as rare as gold, you know that, right?" Avery asked, as if Katie wasn't smart enough to figure that out for herself . . . which was almost true. It had just taken her a bit of time to see what she could potentially lose.

"I pushed him away. Hard," she admitted after swallowing a bite of her lemon cake. "I just . . . panicked. I had horrible flashbacks of my parents' hellish divorce, and all the guys in my past who never stuck around, and I suppose a part of me just felt like I wasn't good enough for a man like Connor."

Avery's mouth literally fell open. "Not good enough? Did he ever make you *feel* that way? Because if so, I'm going to have to kick his ass."

Katie laughed. "No, never." All she'd ever felt with Connor was beautiful and alive and happier than she could ever remember. "Even as I was pushing him away to protect my heart, I knew it was already too late, that I'd already fallen in love with him. I was just too scared to put it out there because it made me feel so vulnerable."

"Oh, honey," Avery said, more gently now. "He's not like all those other jerks you've dated. You know that, right?"

"Of course I know that," she replied without an ounce of doubt in her voice. "I knew that when I ended things, too, but everything happened so fast between us, and it was so intense, that I kept waiting for it to all fall apart, because it always has before. I thought it'd be easier to make a break now, rather than months down the road, but God, I miss him so much."

"So, what are you going to do about it?"

Avery took a drink of her tea, eyeing Katie over the rim for those few seconds before she put her glass down again. "You *are* going to do something, right?"

"I want to . . ."

"But?"

"What if I hurt him too badly, and he doesn't feel the same way any longer?" she asked on a rush of breath, before she lost the nerve, because that was one fear that was still lingering inside her.

Avery burst out laughing. "Are you freakin' blind, Katie? Yes, you probably hurt him when you pushed him away, but your baby daddy is the least egotistical guy I've ever met. I've seen him standing at your door while he picks up Val or drops her off, and the way he looks at you . . . Jesus, you *are* freakin' blind because everything about his body language tells me he's just *waiting* for the day that you finally come to your senses and give him the chance he deserves."

Katie thought back to everything Connor had said to her, the sincere words he'd spoken coming easily because she'd not only memorized them but she replayed them in her head every night while her mind played a game of *what if.* Most specifically, what if she'd trusted him with her heart that day . . . and the answer was always the same. She'd be happy, she'd be in love, and the three of them would be a family. How could she have ever doubted that it would be any other way?

The doorbell rang, and Katie's heart began a heavy, nervous beat inside of her chest because it was most likely Connor and Val. She looked at Avery, who gave her an understanding smile.

"It's now or never," her friend said, as if she knew exactly what Katie had been thinking. "For now, don't obsess about the future. Just take one day at a time with Connor. Let him show you exactly what kind of man he is, and let yourself believe you're worth everything he has to offer you, and Val."

"Okay," she said, and stood, her stomach now joining in on the bout of nervous jitters.

Avery gave her a hug, then looked into Katie's eyes as she offered her last bit of support. "Trust me, you've got this."

Together, they walked through the living room and when Katie opened the door, Avery immediately looked down at Val and said, "Hey, kiddo. Want to come over and play with Leah? And have dinner with us, too?"

"Yeah!" Val said enthusiastically. "Can I, Mommy?"

"Sure. Have fun, and be good," Katie said as the two of them were already hand in hand and heading down the walkway toward Avery's.

Which left her and Connor standing on opposite sides of the door, awkwardly alone since Val had been their buffer for the past week and a half.

"I guess I'll go," he said, but before he could turn around, Katie grabbed his arm to stop him. A slight confused frown formed on his brow as he looked at her. "Everything okay?"

"Yes . . . no . . . " Oh, God, she was already a blabbering mess "I was hoping you could come inside and we could talk for a few minutes?"

"About Val?" he asked, because that's all they'd really discussed since that morning.

She shook her head and swallowed to ease the sudden dryness in her throat. "No, about . . . us."

That frown of his remained in place as he hesitated a moment, just long enough for a wealth of doubts to swirl through her before he put her out of her misery. "Okay."

He walked into the house, and she shut the door behind him. They were in the small living room, a few feet apart with him staring at her as he waited for her to speak, and all she could think was, how in the world did she ease into this conversation? And then it came to her.

"I wanted to tell you that I'm sorry about everything that happened that morning," she said, knowing he didn't need clarification of which morning she was referring to. "For the crazy way I reacted and for pushing you away and for doubting everything you said to me. It was so wrong."

"You don't owe me an apology for the way you feel," he said, his voice a little gruff and uncertain.

She bit her bottom lip as she prepared to take that leap of faith with him. "Yes, I do, because I was wrong, and my issue was, *is*, that I feel so much for you it scares me to death."

"I know," he said simply, the look in his eyes softening, but he remained right where he was, when she wanted so badly for him to close the distance between them.

So, she continued, wanting everything out there—her fears, her insecurities, the doubts she never, ever should have had about him.

"You were right . . . it was easier in that moment to just let you go instead of risking getting hurt."

"And now?"

She couldn't stop her hands from twisting anxiously in front of her. "And now, I know how much it hurts *not* to have you in my life. And how much it hurts to be in love with someone, *with you*, and being so scared that I might have totally screwed everything up."

The corner of his mouth twitched imperceptibly, and he raised a dark, challenging brow. "Say that again, Katie," he ordered softly.

There was no doubt in her mind what part he wanted her to repeat, and she did so with every bit of the emotion that was trying to burst free from her. "I love you, Connor. So much."

With a relieved groan, he walked the steps it took to reach her and immediately pulled her into his arms. "Jesus Christ, Katie," he said against her ear, his own voice rough with joy. "It took you long enough to figure it out."

"I know, and that's why I'm sorry," she said against his strong, muscled chest as she squeezed her arms tight around him. "Because I should have known right then and there that you are a man of your word, that when you say you're in it for the long haul, you mean it."

He pulled back slightly, just enough to take her face between his hands so he could look into her eyes. "Baby, I'm rock solid, and don't you *ever* forget that. I don't give up, and I'm not going anywhere, ever. I love you, and when you're ready, I'm going to marry you."

She couldn't stop the tears that filled her eyes, and did her best to blink them back. "I want to be yours, Connor. I want to be a family with you and Val. I want it all," she said, trusting him completely, without any fears.

A big grin spread across his handsome face. "Ahhh, I like it when you're greedy."

She laughed at the sexual innuendo in his voice. "That's what you get for being so good at everything you do."

"Hmm." Desire flickered in his darkening gaze as he brought his hands down to her ass, then a little lower to her thighs. "How long before Val gets home?" he asked as he effortlessly lifted her, and she automatically wrapped her legs around his waist, their minds already back in sync.

"Oh, a few hours," she said, anticipation in her voice as he started down the hall toward her bedroom.

"Perfect," he murmured, the heat in his eyes making her breathless. "We have a lot of lost time to make up for."

She agreed, and as he pushed her back on the bed and came over her, his mouth hot and hungry on hers and his hands slowly stripping away her clothes so he could worship every inch of her, Katie let herself be loved by the man who would always have her back, take care of her and their child, and most importantly never, ever leave.

Epilogue

One year later . . .

KATIE STOOD OUT on the large patio of the new home she and Connor had recently bought together, watching all their friends and family as they enjoyed the afternoon festivities at Val's fourth birthday party.

Connor's mother and father were there, laughing as Val tore through all the gifts everyone had spoiled her with. His business partners and wives were all present, as well, along with the three new babies each of them had had. Katie had already held and cuddled them all, and it was hard not to catch baby fever from all the sweet cuteness overload.

She glanced down at the huge diamond ring on her finger, the one that Connor had put there on Valentine's Day, which had been the day they'd decided to get married. It had been a small, intimate affair at Connor's parents' house—with Val standing in as the flower girl and throwing rose petals everywhere.

So much had changed in one year, but the things that mattered the most had stayed the same, while other things had grown exponentially. Like Connor's love for her and Val, for one thing. And the fact that she and Val now had a family that they belonged to. There was one other thing that was about to change, as well, but that was a surprise she wanted to share with Connor later, when it was just the three of them.

After a few hours, the party ended, and after everyone was gone and everything cleaned up, Katie went to her office to retrieve the present she'd wrapped earlier, then went back to the kitchen, where Connor was drying the last of the dishes, then handing them to Val to put away.

The two of them were adorable together, and their affection for one another always made Katie smile. Once upon a time, she never would have believed that her heart could feel so full, but Connor had made it possible. She and Val were very lucky girls, and she hoped the gift she was about to give Connor would make him feel just as fortunate.

"Hey, you two," she said, grabbing their attention as she walked into the kitchen with her hands, and the present, behind her back. "I know it's your birthday today, Val, but I have a special present for Daddy, too."

"What is it?" she asked, running over to check out the small wrapped package Katie was now holding in front of her.

Katie grinned at her daughter's impatience. "We're going to find out as soon as Daddy opens it." She handed the long flat box to Connor, who gave her a curious grin.

"Can't imagine what it is," he said, examining the box and the nondescript paper it was wrapped in. "I have everything I could ever want right here in this room."

Katie rolled her eyes at him, though she was smiling. "Trust me, you're going to want this. And just so you know, it can't be returned."

Val jumped up and down beside Connor. "Open it quick, Daddy. I wanna know what it is!"

"Hold your horses, princess," he said as he tore away the wrapping, then lifted the lid on the box.

He had to fold back the tissue paper to find what Katie had put inside, and she watched as he looked at the long plastic stick in confusion, which quickly morphed into shock as he raised his eyes back to her face.

"Is this what I think it is?" he asked, his voice already husky with emotion.

She shrugged, her own throat getting tight at the reverent look in his eyes. "Depends on what you think it is."

"You're pregnant?" His tone was a combination of hope and disbelief. "Already?"

She laughed, because they'd just recently decided to try for a second child now that they were married and settled in a new house. Like, in the past month kind of recent. "What can I say? You have really strong swimmers," she said, keeping things age appropriate since Val was still in the room with them.

Connor set the box on the counter and pulled her into a hug, his warm, strong body enveloping hers. "Just when I think I can't get any luckier than I already am, you prove me wrong all over again."

"What is it?" Val asked enthusiastically. "What did Mommy get you for a present?"

"I am *so* going to thank you for this present later, when we're alone in bed and you're completely naked," he whispered wickedly in her ear. "I might even thank you a *couple* of times," he promised meaningfully before releasing her and turning his attention to his daughter.

He picked Val up so she was sitting on his muscled forearm. "You know that baby brother or sister you keep asking for?"

Val nodded.

"You're going to have one, very soon," he told her.

The little girl's eyes widened. "Yay!" she cheered, clapping her hands happily. "I can't wait!"

Neither could Katie, but as she'd learned over the years since first meeting Connor that snowy night in Denver, some things were definitely worth waiting for.

Thank you for reading ROCK SOLID. We hope you enjoyed Connor and Katie's story! We would appreciate it if you would help others enjoy this book by leaving a review at your preferred e-tailer. Thank you!

ALL BOOKS AVAILABLE IN THE
BOOK BOYFRIEND SERIES:
Big Shot
Faking It
Well Built
Rock Solid

Sign up for Carly Phillips & Erika Wilde's Newsletters:

Carly's Newsletter
http://smarturl.it/CarlysNewsletter

Erika's Newsletter
http://smarturl.it/ErikaWildeNewsletter

ABOUT THE AUTHORS

CARLY PHILLIPS

Carly Phillips is the *N.Y. Times* and *USA Today* Bestselling Author of over 50 sexy contemporary romance novels featuring hot men, strong women and the emotionally compelling stories her readers have come to expect and love. Carly is happily married to her college sweetheart, the mother of two nearly adult daughters and three crazy dogs (two wheaten terriers and one mutant Havanese) who star on her Facebook Fan Page and website. Carly loves social media and is always around to interact with her readers. You can find out more about Carly at www.carlyphillips.com.

ERIKA WILDE

Erika Wilde is the author of the sexy Marriage Diaries series and The Players Club series. She lives in Oregon with her husband and two daughters, and when she's not writing you can find her exploring the beautiful Pacific Northwest. For more information on her upcoming releases, please visit website at erikawilde.com.

Made in the USA
San Bernardino, CA
14 November 2017